UPCHUCK SUMMER

UPCHUCK SUMMER

Joel L. Schwartz
Illustrated by Bruce Degen

A YEARLING BOOK

Published by
Dell Publishing Co., Inc.
1 Dag Hammarskjold Plaza
New York, New York 10017

Yearling ® TM 913705, Dell Publishing Co., Inc.

ISBN: 0-440-49264-5

Reprinted by arrangement with Delacorte Press
Printed in the United States of America

May 1983

10 9 8 7 6 5 4 3

CW

For Nana and Popop and Mitch—
They knew when to listen
and when to speak.

UPCHUCK
SUMMER

Sometimes parents can be pretty stupid. For example, here's what happened last week.

I was talking to my friend Paul on the phone and he was telling me about this kid in his class who was an A-Number-One Nerd, and my mother yells in from the kitchen and asks, "What's a nerd?" I wanted to yell back, "Look it up in the dictionary," since that's what she always tells me to do when I don't know what a word means. But, instead, I yelled back, "A nerd is a turkey," and I continued on with my conversation.

Suddenly, my mother was standing in front of me

with a copy of some college dictionary in her hand and she begins to read aloud.

" 'Turkey: either of two large American gallinaceous birds constituting the genus *Meleagris,* especially *M. gallopavo,* which is domesticated in most parts of the world and esteemed for eating . . .' "

Paul was getting impatient on the other end of the line and began to yell, "Hey, Richie, are you still there? What's going on?"

"Listen, Paul," I said, "I'll call you right back."

With that I slammed down the phone. My mother seemed undaunted by the noise of the phone crashing onto the cradle. She continued: " 'For unrelated similar birds, see Australian turkey, brush turkey, and water turkey.' It doesn't say anything here about a turkey being a nerd."

"But, Mom, you don't understand. A turkey is a clod."

"A clod? What's a clod?"

"A clod is a spaz."

"A spaz? What's a spaz?"

"A spaz is a nerd."

"What language are you talking about?" she asked.

I wanted to tell her I was talking in an ancient Nerdonian dialect used by Babylonian teen-agers who didn't want their parents to understand their phone conversations. But, instead, I said in a very disgusted voice: "I am speaking English; I have always spoken English; I will continue to speak English."

No sooner had the sentence come out of my mouth, than I realized that it would have probably been better to say that Babylonian thing.

"Listen," snapped my mother, "don't you talk fresh to me. I just asked you a simple question, and I deserve a simple answer."

I hung my head, giving the appearance of repentance, knowing that would be the only way to get rid of her.

"I haven't liked your language lately, anyway," she continued. "You better shape up or I'll . . ."

Yeah, I know, I said to myself. *You'll talk to my father who uses much better language than I. Would you prefer I use Dad's four-letter words instead of nerd or turkey, huh?*

My forlorn look obviously worked because she stopped barking at me and returned to the kitchen.

In order to continue my call in the privacy it de-

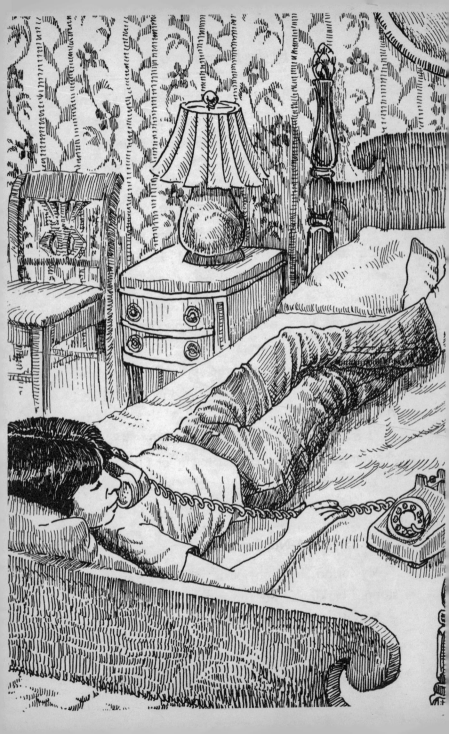

served, I decided to go upstairs to the seclusion of my parents' room. I don't know why, but I must get into the same position every time I use the phone in this room, otherwise things just don't seem right. So I lay sort of on my back and sort of on my side, my feet crossed left over right, resting on the pillow at the top of the bed, while my head just touched the footboard below.

"What happened?" said Paul.

"Did you know that a turkey is one of two gallinaceous birds constituting the genus *Meleagris*?"

"What the hell are you talking about?" interrupted Paul.

That's great. When I talk like my mother wants, my friends don't understand me. When I talk like my friends want, my mother doesn't understand me.

"Oh, forget it," I said. "What were we talking about before we were interrupted?"

"I forget," said Paul. "Let's see . . ."

"Nerd!" we both said in unison.

"That little A-Number-One Nerd, Chuck."

"What about him?" I questioned.

"You're not going to like this," said Paul. "But

5

today I found out at lunch that Chuck is going to be at camp with you."

"Oh, no! How did you find out?"

"You remember that hat you got the first year you signed up at camp? Well, Chuck was wearing one today in school. During second lunch we grabbed it and we were playing keep-away and he begged us not to get his new camp hat dirty. I told him you went to that camp and you would be glad to answer any questions he might have."

"You told him what!" I said in disbelief. "I would answer what, who!"

"Only kidding," said Paul.

"Very funny," I said. "Nice guy you are.

"Hey, by the way, how was old man Singer's math test? We get it tomorrow."

"Not bad," said Paul. "Twenty integer problems just like the ones you did for homework."

"Richie, get off the phone. You've been on long enough."

That old familiar sound from downstairs.

"One more minute, Mom."

"No more minutes. You have homework to do."

"I only have a little bit tonight," I yelled, knowing very well what the response would be.

"Richie, now!"

"Hey, listen, Paul, I have to hang up. I'll call you later."

As I hung up the phone and walked into my room, I wished that sometime I would be the one to tell my mother to hang up.

"Excuse me, Mrs. Harmon, but you have been on the phone for seven hours. It is time to make dinner."

"One more hour, please."

"No more hours. Now!"

I flopped, stomach down, on my bed and propped my math book up against my pillow.

"Richie, come down here," my mother called again. "I want to talk to you."

I wish she would make up her mind. First she says do homework and then she says come down. Mothers seem to do that a lot. Last weekend she told my father he was working too hard and he should rest. So over the weekend he sits down to watch a baseball game and she tells him he has to put in the screens.

"What do you want, Mom," I yelled back.

"Come down here. I don't like to yell," she said.

I closed my math book and slowly went down into the kitchen. A stack of dishes piled high on the drain board caught my eye, and I knew immediately what my fate would be.

"Do I have to?" I said. "I have so much homework to do. I'll be up all hours tonight."

"Then how do you have time to talk on the telephone?" I knew I was a dead duck. I began to dry.

"Guess who called me today asking about camp?" she said.

Oh, no, it's true. Chuck's mother called.

"I give up," I said, with a puzzled look on my face. "Who called?"

"Mrs. Collins. Chuck is going to be at camp with you this summer. Won't that be nice?"

"No," I said emphatically. "I hate him."

"What did he ever do to you?"

It's no use. She will never understand.

"Chuck is such a nice boy, and he comes from such a nice family."

Then you go to camp with him.

Sometimes I knew when to keep my mouth shut.

God must have had it in for some kids, and Chuck Collins was one of them. He was short, wore glasses, and was poor in sports. What a lousy combination. From the very first time I met him last May after his family moved into the neighborhood, I knew he was a loser. Some kids have that tease me, trip me, give me a noogie on the head look on their face, and Chuck was one of them. He was a nerd, a clod, a turkey, a spaz, a leech, an itch.

"Uh, what did he ever do to you?" my mother repeated.

"Nothing," I said.

"Then why don't you like him?"

"Because."

"Why don't you like him? There must be a reason."

"I don't know," I mumbled. Sometimes, mostly when I'm questioned, sentences just don't come out. I try to answer, but all I can manage is one or two words like nothing, because, I don't know.

The dishes were done so I threw the towel on the counter and walked up to my room. I think my mother was still firing questions, but I really wasn't paying attention. I flopped down on the bed again and started to look at my math. I heard the rumbling patter of my younger brother and sister coming up the stairs. I kicked my door shut to keep them out. I still couldn't believe that Chuck was going to camp with me, but I did know one thing for sure: There was absolutely no way that Chuck was going to sit next to me on the bus ride up.

2

Everybody says that when you grow up, you are able to make decisions for yourself. For instance, this year the seventh grade got to decide where they wanted to go on their class trip. So on Thursday seventh period was canceled. And we all filed into the auditorium. If I had only known, I could have watched TV last night instead of studying. Since you didn't have to stay with the group you came in with, I looked for Paul and found him already sitting down.

"Did you save me a seat?" I yelled. He nodded.

I slid down the center aisle and was just about to turn into the row when Mrs. Fletcher grabbed me by the arm and told me to behave. "Okay," I said, but I continued sliding the rest of the way the minute she turned her back. When I got halfway into the row, my feet became tangled up with somebody else's, and before I knew it, I had fallen right onto Chuck Collins's lap.

"Why don't you watch your damn feet?" I said, as I glared at him.

"Gee, Richie. I'm sorry," said Chuck. "I didn't mean it."

I stood up and raised my hand just to see Chuck flinch.

"You wimp," I said, and all the boys around me cheered.

Then I noticed that the chair Paul had saved for me was right next to Chuck, so I said loudly, "I ain't sit'n' next to this queer!" Another cheer from the crowd and I started to leave the row.

"Richie," yelled Mrs. Fletcher. "Having trouble finding a seat?"

"No," I said. "There is one right here." I sat down next to Chuck.

Elmer Fudd—our principal, Mr. Lynch—was now standing at the front of the auditorium waiting. "I'm not going to begin until everyone is

quiet," he bellowed. "Today we are meeting to decide where you will go on your seventh-grade class
trip. The floor is open for suggestions."

One girl sitting in the front row raised her hand
and said, "How about the art museum?" Most of the
boys, me included, booed and stamped our feet. Mr.
Lynch banged his fist down loudly on the podium.

"If you children don't know how to behave, I'll
just dismiss you and there will be no trip."

Fat chance.

Then a kid from one of the lower sections yelled
out, "How about Belmont Amusement Park?" We
all cheered and stamped our feet.

Lynchie was pounding harder and threatening
again, so we got back down to business. After that
some of the suggestions that were made were ex-
cellent: New York—a trip to the UN, lunch, and a
show. Washington—some monuments, lunch, and
the White House. Williamsburg—the restored vil-
lage, lunch, and Busch Gardens.

Mr. Lynch said he would think about all of these
wonderful suggestions and let us know on Monday.

On the way out of the auditorium, Paul and I
and a couple of the other guys were talking, and I

happened to look over my shoulder and saw Chuck walking about ten yards behind us all by himself. I wouldn't tell anybody else this, but for an instant I sort of felt sorry for him and a little ashamed of my behavior. But I wouldn't tell anybody else that because if the other guys knew that, they might think I was a . . . but I'm not, so I quickly dismissed the thought.

Monday came around and guess where Mr. Lynch told us we were going to go? To the Mint. Every year I hear the seventh-grade class goes to the Mint, so why even ask us? My parents do that to me too. They will ask me, "What do you want to do this summer?" "Well," I say, "I'm tired of going to camp and I want to stay home." "There is nothing at all to do here," they say. "You are going to camp."

There was one thing, however, that seventh-grade boys had full power to decide, and there seemed to be a fifty-fifty split over the issue: Should I or should I not take a shower after gym? To a parent that may seem like a very simple question. "If you are dirty or smell bad, you should take a shower." But parents always seem to make simple questions complicated and complicated questions simple.

Until the beginning of this year I would never have done it. Never in a million years. And if you were to ask me why, I would have answered, "There wasn't enough time," or "The shower room was dirty," or "There was only cold water," or some other excuse. But they weren't the real reasons. The real reason was that I was embarrassed to be naked in front of other boys because I was sure everyone was more developed than me. You know, there are certain touchy subjects that I couldn't talk to anyone about, not even Paul, and this was one of them. Once or twice when I was at the library, supposedly getting information for my science report on the digestive system, I tried to look for some books that might help. I found a couple that looked like they had some information in them, but they were written in such big words, I couldn't understand a thing. Maybe when I grow up I'll write a simple book or just make a chart telling boys my age how many hairs they should have in certain places at certain ages or how big their thing should be. It would sure help. However, with nothing to go on, I was left only to compare in my mind, and naturally I came up short. Occasionally, well, maybe every other night, I would look at myself in the mirror to see if there had been any changes. I would often hear the doctor tell my mother, "He is going to be at least six feet. Look at how long his legs are." Or a neighbor say, "He is going to be tall. Look at how big his feet are." Nevertheless, I saw myself in sixth grade as a four foot, ten inch hairless midget, with long legs and big feet. I was determined to change my disgusting shape. So I sent away for a special book written by the world's foremost expert in body building. I did the exercises religiously and sort of followed this special diet that was located at the back of the book. I found that at the end of sixth grade, I was a five foot hairless midget, with long muscular legs and big feet. But over that summer things began to change. By the time school started, I was five feet, one and a half inches and growing. But I'm not sure if I would have been ready to take a group shower if it hadn't have been for Paul.

"Are you a chicken?" he said.

"Look who is calling who a chicken," I said. "Are you going to do it?"

"I will if you will," said Paul.

"Okay, meet me at my locker after gym and we will get undressed together."

For some reason I didn't trust Paul, and I wasn't going in there alone. But after gym Paul was there and we quickly undressed. Whistling proudly, we threw our towels over our shoulders and walked to the shower room.

The room was set up like a horseshoe so you could put your towel at one end and start at the other. I paused at the beginning, thinking that I might say I had to go to the bathroom and then run back and get dressed, but the oncoming crowd carried us forward. Hunching over as I soaped myself up, I began to notice some of the other boys. To my surprise most of them looked the same as me. In fact, I think I looked better. I began to feel very proud and I straightened up to show myself off when I was suddenly hit in the face with a wet towel. I looked around to see who did it, and everyone was pointing at somebody else. I flung the towel into a crowd. Soon there were two towels and then five, and people slipping and falling on top of each other. Suddenly we heard Coach Watson's whistle.

He was standing at the end of the horseshoe yelling for everybody to get out. All of us grabbed our towels, and laughing hysterically, we ran back to our lockers.

I learned two things that day. One, never turn your back on anyone in the shower, and two, I forget what the second one was.

3

If anybody came into my mother's room right now they would surely think I was crazy. You see, I was saying good-bye to Paul because tomorrow I was going to camp, and we were smack in the middle of our last belching contest for over two months.

"That was a pretty good one, Paul," I said, "but listen to this."

I took three deep gulps of air, threw back my neck, and out came "BREECHCH, BREECHCH, UG, BREC, a triple." I said.

"Richie, are you all right?" said my mother, knocking on the locked door.

"I'm fine, Mom."

"Are you sure? It sounded like you were vomiting."

"No, I'm fine. I'm just saying good-bye to Paul."

"Make the call short," she said. "You know you have to get up early."

"Listen, Paul, you do have my address, don't you? Write to me when you get a chance. I'll keep you posted on Chuck."

"Have a nice summer," said Paul. "BREECH, BREECH, BREECH, BREECH, a quadruple, I win."

"Hey, that's not fair," I said. "I thought the contest was over. You son of a . . . BREECH, BREECH, BREECH, BREECH, another quadruple. It's a tie."

"Don't get too much," said Paul.

"Don't do anything I wouldn't do," I said. "And that gives you a lot of leeway. So long."

"So long," said Paul.

I sat on the edge of the bed for a second.

"BREECH, BREECH, BREECH, BREECH, BREECH." A quintuple! But too late for the competition.

When I finished in the bathroom, I went to my room and undressed and was just about to go to sleep when my father appeared. He sat down on the bed beside me, and I knew all too well what he was going to say.

"Richie, I won't be able to go to the bus with you tomorrow, so I wanted to say good-bye to you tonight."

It's difficult to look attentive year after year, but I tried my best. My father is an okay guy, although he has gotten a little obnoxious over the past six months. He tries too hard to be one of the guys with my friends. It's a funny thing though—my friends think he is great, while I think their fathers are great and they think their fathers are obnoxious.

When he finished his speech, he bent over and gave me a hug, which seemed nice for a second, but then made me feel like a little kid, so I pulled away and stuck out my hand.

"No more hugs," I said. "Just handshakes."

My father obliged without a word, and he got up and turned out the light on his way out. I closed my eyes and tried desperately to fall asleep. Thoughts about this season at camp swirled through my head, and I found myself tossing and turning for what seemed like an eternity. Finally I sat up in bed and said softly to myself, "I can't fall asleep. It's been hours that I have been rolling around." I looked at the clock and realized that only ten minutes had passed. So I lay back down and sometime after that I fell asleep.

I wish my parents would make up their minds. Last night at dinner I asked for a fourth helping of steak, but my parents said, "Richie, you've been eating too much lately. You've had enough." So I decided that since I had been eating too much lately, I wasn't going to have breakfast today. But my mother said, "You can't leave the house for the camp bus unless you eat a good breakfast."

"I'm not that hungry," I said.

"Me neither," said Robby, who's eleven.

Sally, who's eight, just stood there and whined.

"It's not healthy to start out the day without a good meal," my mother replied.

Personally, I would rather have had the extra piece of steak last night and skipped the mushy cereal today.

"I'm really not that hungry, Mom," I said again.

"I'm really not that hungry," echoed Robby.

"Speak for yourself," I said, glaring at Robby.

"I am speaking for myself," said Robby.

"No breakfast, no camp," said my mother.

"Okay," I said, "juice, cereal, and toast."

"Juice, cereal, and toast," echoed Robby.

"Can't you think for yourself?" I said.

"I was going to say that before you. So there!"

"So there," was my brother's greatest weapon. It was supposed to be a great comeback and put-down.

"And what do you want for breakfast?" said my mother, putting her arm around Sally.

"I want, sniff sniff, some juice, sniff sniff, cereal, sniff, and toast," sniffed Sally.

My sister should get an Academy Award for Best Performance by Pain-in-the-Neck Sister at the last meal before going to camp.

The other day my friend Paul told me a good joke that reminded me of my sister.

What did the grape say when the elephant stepped on it? Answer: It whined a little.

A good belt in the mouth would straighten her out. I don't know if anybody will ever date her, but if they do, I'll be sure to tell them what a pain she is.

After breakfast I grabbed my things and yelled for my mom to get going.

"I just want to do the breakfast dishes before I leave," she said.

"But, Ma, we'll be late."

"I can't leave the house in such bad condition," she said.

At that point I threw my things down and began to pace. What great laws of the universe would be violated if a few dirty dishes were left in the sink? Suddenly a strange, deep voice from the back of my mind bellowed, "The following are laws never to be violated. One, no one is ever to leave the house unless all the dishes are done and put away. Two, no one is ever to leave the house unless all the beds are made. Three, no one is ever to leave the house unless their room is clean. Four, no one is ever to go to bed unless they shower. Do not, I repeat, do not forget to wash your face and behind your ears. Five, no one is ever to go to Grandmother's house without changing their clothes and washing or showering. Six, no one is ever, I repeat, no one is ever . . ."

"Richie, what are you staring at?" my mother asked. "Come on, let's go or we'll be late."

4

If parents can have unwritten rules that must be followed, then kids can too. One that comes to mind is that the back seat of all the buses is reserved for the oldest boys, and this year that means me. A couple of years ago an eleven-year-old boy who thought he was cool refused to move from there, so the oldest boy stripped his bed fifteen times, stole his underwear, dumped lake water in his bed, and generally made his life so miserable he left camp at the first visiting day. It is a great feeling to know that you've finally arrived at the back and will be given the respect you deserve.

"Don't forget to write," my mother said.

"I won't."

"Don't get into trouble."

"I won't."

"Don't get hurt."

"I won't."

"Look after your brother and sister."

"I won't."

"Richie, are you paying attention to me? Lately you seem in a world of your own."

"I won't, Mom. Hey, look, I gotta go. Good-bye."

As I took off in the direction of the bus, I heard footsteps and I turned to see Robby following stride for stride, close behind. He slowed his pace when he saw me look, but seemed to speed up when I turned around. They say it's supposed to be an honor when a younger brother imitates you, but frankly, I think it's a pain.

I got on the bus, and I knew that everyone was watching me jealously as I moved slowly toward the back seat.

"Hey, Richie," three guys yelled in unison. "How are you?"

"Tom, John, Fred, you queers," I yelled back. "How are you?"

"Great," they replied. "Come on back, we saved you a seat."

"Who is that weirdo?" asked Tom, pointing to the front of the bus.

I turned and saw Chuck getting on. He was wearing long, baggy blue shorts, high white socks, and yellow sneakers with a white star on the back. In his hand he carried a case with a picture of Spiderman.

"Why don't his parents get better clothes for him," I thought.

"That weirdo is Chuck Collins," I said, somewhat loudly.

I like Spiderman too, but I would never carry a bag with his picture on it. I bet he has a lunch box and a thermos with Spiderman on them.

"He ain't going to sit back here with us," I said.

Someone, but not me, ought to straighten Chuck out.

"There's no room here," chimed in John.

"All filled," said Fred.

Chuck looked back at me for a second as if he had heard. He took a seat next to my sister behind the bus driver.

"A perfect pair," I said. "A wimp and a whiner!"

The boys in the back seat roared at that one.

The atmosphere was electric. The little kids were either crying or yelling, and the older girls tried, somewhat successfully, to lead the bus in song.

"BINGO, BINGO, BINGO, and Bingo was his name-o. B-I-N-G, clap, B-I-N-G, clap, B-I-N-G, clap, and Bingo was his name-o."

In between flashing obscene gestures to the passing motorists or the people eating at Howard Johnson's, I swapped stories with the other guys. I hadn't seen them for almost a year. It was like a contest of who could tell the wildest, supposedly true story. I don't think any of the stories were true, I know mine wasn't, but I said it was true for sure and they did too.

"Listen to this," I said. "An older guy I know has been going with this girl for a long time, and they decide they are going to make out in the nude on her birthday. The birthday part is important so don't forget it. This guy goes to the girl's house, and after her parents leave, they go upstairs and get undressed. A short time later the phone rings and it's the girl's

father. He tells her that he thinks he left some rags near the heater and he is afraid there will be a fire and could she check it out for him. They both decide that it's too much trouble to put on their clothes, so the girl gets on her boyfriend's back, piggyback, and they go downstairs. When they get to the basement, the boyfriend puts on the light and everybody yells 'Surprise!' ''

"Surprise?" said Fred.

"Surprise! You dummy," I said. "They were giving her a surprise party."

"And the boyfriend didn't know about it?" asked Fred again.

"Oh, forget it," I said.

"Wait, I have one too," said John. "This couple goes to a honeymoon resort. You know, heart-shaped bathtubs, heart-shaped beds. Well they have a cable TV system. The first night the couple is tired and they don't watch TV at all. The next night they turn on the TV and guess what they see? Themselves from the night before."

"I don't believe that," Tom said. "Who took the pictures?"

"Yeah," chimed in Fred. "Where was the micro-phone?"

"Who wrote the script?" I said. "I think that's a lot of bull."

"Well, I think your story was a lot of bull too, if you want to know the truth," said John.

"Oh, yeah, well then . . ."

"Hey, guys," Fred said, "break it up. We're coming up to Howard Johnson's and there's an old couple sitting in the window. Let's get ready to shake up their lunch."

"We're here because we're here, because we're here, because we're here. We're here because we're here, because we're here, because we're here."

Everyone got off the buses and piled into the rec hall to find out what bunk they would be in and who their counselors would be. For me it was no mystery. The oldest boys are always in a bunk called "The Club" and their counselor is always Mike. Nevertheless, we still had to go in and listen to Uncle Oscar, the camp director, give his speech and introduce the counselors and staff. It reminded me of the first day at school when the principal met with the new students. I pictured Elmer Fudd in a T-shirt and shorts standing up in front of the student body and I chuckled.

The oldest boys sat in the last two rows. We tried to spread out so Chuck couldn't get a seat, but one of the new counselors insisted that we move over and let him sit down. Well, as luck would have it, not too long after Chuck joined us, someone, not me, let one go. An S.B.D. (Silent But Deadly). By the time the smell got to me, half of the row in front of me was coughing and pretending to gag.

"You did it," said Tom, pointing to Fred.

"Not me," said Fred. "It was John."

"Not me," said John. "It was Chuck."

By that time we were all pointing at Chuck with our right hands while holding our noses with our left hands and chanting, "Chuck did it! Chuck did it!"

"Not me," said Chuck. "I didn't do it. Not me."

"Chuck did it! Chuck did it!"

Tweet, tweet, tweet, went Oscar's whistle and we all got quiet.

"What's going on?"

"They think I laid a fa—" said Chuck, but he stopped when he realized what he was about to say. "Nothing."

"What's a fa?" said Oscar.

"Nothing," said Chuck, hanging his head.

We had to hold our mouths to prevent ourselves from bursting out laughing.

From that day on, at least once a day, one of the guys would go over to Chuck and say, " 'Doe, a deer a female deer. Ray, a drop of golden sun. Me, a name I call myself. Fa, a, oh, nothing.' "

5

It was impossible for anything to go wrong. For weeks I had spent at least part of my social studies periods making plans instead of listening to Mrs. Poole babble on about the Civil War. Timing was important. If I started to leave the rec hall too early, I would be made to come back and wait for everybody else to go, but if things were just right, I could be out of the rec hall and on my way to the bunk before anyone else. My objective was to get the best bed in the bunk, and nothing could stop me now. Nothing except stepping in a hole on the lawn. As I fell in a heap with my packages flying in all directions, I saw my bunkmates racing past and my plans going down the drain. I picked myself up slowly and brushed the grass off the scrape on my left knee. There was no use rushing now. No one was in sight. I felt a little like crying, somewhat out of embarrassment, but mostly out of anger. I started to pick up my packages. For a second I wanted to go home, then I wished I could roll back the clock in order to race to the bunk again, without falling. You know how your mind begins to think bad things, and once it starts, it doesn't seem to stop? That's what was happening to me now.

Guess what bed you are going to end up with? The stinkiest, smelliest bed in the bunk. The one next to the bathroom. The smell will be so bad you won't be able to sleep, and if you can't sleep, you will get run down and not be able to play your best when you try out for the camp team. And you probably won't get picked for any teams and no one will like you if you are not on any teams and your summer will be ruined and, and . . .

I looked around to make sure I had picked up everything, and I limped slowly to the bunk. I really didn't have to limp, but I felt sorry for myself. Nobody seemed to pay attention to me when I came in, and only a few looked up when I threw my packages on the floor with a thud. I kicked my stuff soccer style toward the only bed left. My worst fears had come true.

"My summer is ruined," I muttered.

No one paid attention.

Okay, guys. Ask me if you can borrow my baseball glove and see what you get.

"What's the matter, Richie?" said Chuck.

"Oh, you wouldn't understand," I said, starting to unpack.

"Why are you so upset?" he persisted.

"Forget it," I snapped, as I returned to my own unpacking.

"Why is Richie so mad?" said Chuck to Fred, who was in the bed next to him.

"No one wants to sleep next to the bathroom," said Fred.

"Why not?" said Chuck.

"Because it stinks and it's noisy and there is no privacy and you always get wet if there is a water fight.

"Oh," said Chuck as he continued making his bed.

In the meantime I was throwing my things into the cubby and banging things around pretty good. I noticed Chuck standing at the end of the bed staring at me.

"What are you looking at?" I bellowed. "Didn't you ever see anyone pissed off before?"

"Richie, do you want to change beds?" said Chuck.

"Hit me with that again," I said.

"I would be glad to change beds with you," said Chuck. "I really don't care where I sleep."

"You want to change beds with me?" I said incredulously.

"I will if you want," he said again.

At first I was puzzled. Not only was he a nerd, but he was also a stupid nerd. No, that couldn't be it because he did do pretty well in school. Slowly it dawned on me. He was trying to get on my good side. He probably thought if he did this for me, then I would be his friend, and if I were his friend, then the other kids in the bunk would be his friend too. It wasn't going to work. I once knew some weird kid in school who spent a lot of money buying gum for a whole mess of kids that he wanted to have as friends. They liked him, or made him think they liked him, as long as the gum lasted. When that disappeared, so did their friendship. Sometimes kids give out half of their sandwich or their whole sandwich or dessert or even their whole lunch, but food and gum don't make permanent friends. Paul once got invited to a basketball game by some creep and he went and said the game was great, but after that he never talked to the kid again. Tickets to sporting events, swimming pools, toys, candy, clothes, and even money never ever work. Somehow when a nerd does something for someone, it never is the same as when a friend does something for someone. That something never changes a nerd into a friend. It never works.

"Here, let me help you carry over your things," said Chuck.

It's not going to work.

"I really don't mind where I sleep," he said again.

It's not going to work.

But Chuck couldn't hear my thoughts so he kept on carrying all my things over to my new bed, and I just sat there thinking, *It's not going to work.*

* * *

That first night everyone in camp was supposed to go to bed early, but our bunk stayed up late talking and telling jokes. I got to thinking about other first nights at camp. I hate to admit this, but I almost became a nerd my first year at camp, and if it weren't for my best friend Fred in the bed next to me, I probably would have become one. We were both seven years old and away from home for the first time. I was pretty homesick and later on Fred told me he was too. Just before the lights went out, that first night, I was sitting on the end of my bed wishing that I could be home with my mommy and daddy. Can you imagine that? Fred had always been a very sensitive guy, and he came over to my bed and sat down next to me.

"Are you always this quiet?" he said.

Only when I am afraid if I talk, I'll cry.

"Sometimes," I said.

"Is that your glove over there?" he asked, pointing to a Larry Bowa model infielder's glove hanging on a hook above my bed.

I'm not sure I like being away from home. Eight weeks is a long time.

"Yeah, that's my glove," I said.

"Can I see it?" asked Fred.

Maybe I could go home tomorrow for a little bit then come back the next day.

"Here," I said, handing it to Fred. "But be careful."

"Boy that really has a great pocket. It's a great glove. Where did you get it?"

Maybe my father could stop by on his way home from work just to say hello, and maybe he could have a catch with me.

"My father got it for my birthday."

"Where do you live?" asked Fred.

Maybe my parents could send me a picture. I could put it on my cubby and look at it when I need to.

"Suburban Philadelphia. Where are you from?"

"Long Island, New York," said Fred. "Boy, this glove is really great, do you want to have a catch with me tomorrow?"

Hey, I would like that.

"I would like that," I said.

"Will you let me use your glove a little? I'll let you use mine."

Hey, this is really nice.

40

"What kind of a glove do you have?"

"Let me get it," said Fred. Then he went back to his bed for a second and returned. "Here, but be careful. I've been working on this pocket for four months."

My pocket is much better than his.

"Boy, that's a great pocket," I said. "Where did you get the glove?"

"My father got it for me," he said. "Look, the lights are out, I'd better go back to my bed. Don't forget tomorrow."

I won't.

"I won't," I said. "See you tomorrow."

If Fred hadn't come over and talked to me and I had cried, then I would have become—I don't even want to think about it. Thank God it didn't happen.

6

"Going to the bathroom again?" asked Fred.

"Are you keeping score?" I asked.

"Well, it's your fourth time already today."

"Fred, do me a favor," I said, "look at your chart and tell me how many times I went last Friday." I went into one of the toilets and slammed the door. One thing I didn't need now was to be bugged by anyone, and the bathroom was a good place to hide. Every inch of wall space was covered with memories of other years and important sayings about life left by philosophers of the past. I loved to read the walls.

"Ron, Bill, Fred, Tom, Tommy, Rich, Eric, Danny, Ralph, Mike, Elvin, Saul, Club 1971."

Mike was my counselor now. A real great guy.

"Judy and Cy 1969 XX."

Never heard of them.

"We aim to keep this bathroom clean, your aim will help."

I once wrote that on a three-by-five card and put it in our powder room at home when my parents were having a big party. My mother had a fit and when my father laughed, my mother got even madder.

"Red 2493—Blue 2492."

This year I hope to be a camper captain for Olympics. Boy, that would be great.

"Richie, it's time to go. Are you coming?"

"One second, Fred, I'll be right out."

"I'm only waiting a minute and if you are not out, I'm going."

"Here I am," I said, appearing from the bathroom with a bow. "What's the rush?"

"Come on and get your glove. Everyone is already at the field."

Our counselor, Mike, was also the coach of our team, and he had just begun to talk to the rest of the guys, who were already seated on the bottom row of the bleachers. Fred and I slipped in quietly behind him.

"This year I expect to have a championship team," he said. "I expect everyone here to give your all during every practice and every game. Today we are going to have tryouts to determine who will start and who will be a sub for the first game, but don't think that just because you start this game means you will start every game. Who wants to start first at pitcher?"

Tom raised his hand.

"Okay, Tom, get to the mound. How about first?"

John and Ed raised their hands.

"Okay, John, you start. Ed, you sit out for a while. Second?"

Only Bill raised his hand. He went out. "Shortstop?"

I raised my hand high and looked around to see if there would be any competition. At first no one raised his hand, but then Marty, one of the new kids, raised his.

"Okay, Richie, you go out and, Marty, you sit down on the bleachers until I tell you to switch."

I picked up my glove and ran out to my position,

glad that I had the first opportunity to show off my stuff. When all the positions were set, Mike began to hit balls to us. I felt a little nervous when the first ground ball came to me, and it squirted through my hands into left field. I kicked the ground in disgust and muttered sounds of encouragement to myself. They seemed to help, for I scooped up the next ground ball and threw it to first. The rest of my first turn was pretty good, and I was a little annoyed when I had to leave the field to let Marty in. As I lay down on the bleachers to wait for my next turn, I watched Marty out of the corner of my eye. He was pretty good. Not as good as I was, but pretty good. I wished he would make one error like me, or maybe even two. I know it's not nice to think that, but I really wanted to start at shortstop. There is a great sense of pride in starting a game or getting a hit or making a great play.

"Richie, your turn again."

"This time there will be no errors," I thought as I ran onto the field. "Just remember, get your body down behind the ball and scoop it up just like this." And with that I scooped up the ball and flung it to first base. "Here comes another one. Ease over to the left. That's right. Great play. Now throw it. Good throw."

"Baseball used to be more fun when I was little," I thought. "But now it is serious business."

In the old days, if I wanted to play ball, I would call two kids who in turn would call two kids, and before you knew it there were enough to have a game. It didn't make any difference what position you played. Everyone seemed to get a chance at each spot except right field. That's where the nerds always played, where they could do the least damage. The game usually lasted until it got too dark to see or until too many players had to go home. Even winning or losing didn't seem as important then. Don't get me wrong, I like winning as well as the next guy, but sometimes now it seems more important to win than to have fun.

"Okay, Richie, sit down. Marty, you're in."

Okay, Marty. Try to match that performance. If I must say so myself, I was great.

I hoped I would get another chance in the field, but I was called up to bat next. I hit about five deep flies to left and five singles, or maybe doubles, up the middle.

"That's all for today," said Mike. "I'll post who is playing what position in the bunk after breakfast tomorrow. Our first game will be Monday."

I hardly ate much breakfast the next day, and as soon as we could leave the dining room, I ran down to the bunk to see the results. Behind the door was a huge sheet of yellow paper.

> Catcher—Jack
> Pitcher—Tom
> First—John
> Second—Bill
> Short—Marty
> Third—Fred
> Left—Steve
> Center—Ron
> Right—Richie
> Substitutes—Chuck, Ed, Danny

I kicked the wall in disgust. And how did I get placed in right field? Anyone knows that the kids that can't catch play right field. I'm not going to play right field.

"Is there something the matter?" said Mike.

"Why can't I play short?"

"Because I thought Marty was a little better."

"If I can't play short, then I don't want to play."

"I think that's a hasty decision, Richie. I think you are good, but only one person can play short, so I put you someplace else where I thought you could help the team."

"I don't want to play right. Only nerds play right."

"The game is not until Monday so think about it," said Mike, as he walked away.

There is nothing to think about, I said to myself. *I ain't going to play.*

7

Monday came and I wasn't playing. I had made up my mind and nothing had changed it yet.

"Ahh, come on, Richie," said Fred. "It's better than sitting on the bench."

"Would you play right field?"

"I'm already playing third base."

"But if you weren't playing third, would you play right?"

"Why ah, sure."

"I ain't doing it!"

"You are an important part of the team," said Mike. "I really wish you would reconsider."

I hung my head.

"I'm not going to play no matter what."

It's not fair. I'm as good as Marty.

"I know you don't think it's fair," said Mike.

How does he know what I think?

"But things can't go your way all the time."

Yeah, I know, but how about going my way this time.

"Sometimes you have to do something you don't want to do."

I'll go for the ride to the other camp, but I'm not playing.

When Mike called for everyone to come to the van I straggled behind a little. By the time I got to the van there was only one seat left. You guessed it! The one next to Chuck.

"Hey, Richie, who's your friend?" said Fred.

I turned around and I gave Fred my shut-up-or-I'll-bust-you-in-the-face look.

Fred shut up.

"Hi, Richie," said Chuck. "I'm really nervous about playing in front of other people. Do you ever get nervous?"

Sure, I get nervous.

"Me get nervous? Not me. I love playing in front of other people. It makes me play better."

I can see that Chuck believed me. I laughed to myself.

"Can I sit next to you on the trip home, Richie?"

"Can I sit next to you on the trip home?" said Tom.

Thank God Mike got up and began to give final instructions. By the time he finished, the van was just arriving at the other camp and I didn't have to answer. The other team was already on the field practicing and they looked mighty big.

As I sat in the bleachers waiting for our turn at practice, I began to think.

This camp really has a nice field. I wonder what it would be like to play on a field like this. Well, I'll never know. Maybe I'll just practice with the team. That's not giving in. Boy, I'd sure like to play today. No, I can't. It would really be fun. No. Maybe just a couple of innings.

Well, when it was time for our team to go onto the field, I stayed back for a second and told Mike I guessed I would play, but only for a couple of innings. Mike didn't say a word, but instead he smacked me on the rear and told me to hustle onto the field. I smiled back at him as I ran.

That Mike's a great guy. I wish I could be like him when I grow up.

Mike had been a camper and he had come up through the ranks to become one of the best-liked counselors. During the winter he was a premedical student at a small college in New York. He wanted to be a heart surgeon.

It seemed to me as if our team got gypped in warm-up time because I barely caught the ball five times when it was time to come in and start the game.

The first inning was fairly short with both sides getting three outs quickly. In the second inning Marty got a single and advanced to second on a fielder's choice. Next Fred hit the ball hard, but it was only a long fly to center. Now it was up to me. I grabbed my favorite bat and walked confidently to the plate. I kicked the dirt back and forth with the heel of my shoe, and after a minute I was finally satisfied that everything was right and I turned to face the pitcher. The first pitch was high and out-side, but I swung wildly, missing it completely. I almost swung at the next pitch, but I was glad I didn't because it bounced two feet in front of the plate. The next two pitches were equally bad. With the count 3 and 1, I knew the pitcher had to come in with something good. He did, but I only got a piece of it and fouled it off to the left. Beads of perspiration formed on my forehead as I waited for the next pitch. It was a little high and a little outside but too close to let go by, so I swung with all my might. I sent it deep into left center field between the two fielders. Marty scored easily and I was safe at third on a close play. I felt about ten feet tall as I stood up to brush myself off while my team cheered, "Richie! Richie! Richie!"

The next time at bat I had a double and the third time a single and I stole second. Unfortunately, these were the only hits our team got. We lost 17 to 1. But I still felt like a hero, and I heard "Richie! Richie! Richie!" over and over in my mind. I knew I was lucky to have played such a spectacular game, and whenever I feel that way, I always want to keep things just the same as they were so as not to spoil my luck. Other people are superstitious like me, but in different ways. Once my brother started to open an umbrella in the house and my grandmother nearly had a fit. To counteract the fact that it was halfway open, my grandmother started to run around the kitchen and throw salt over her shoulder. A friend at home told me that one time when he was on vacation with his family they were given a room on the thirteenth floor of some hotel and his parents refused to take it.

My thing was that everything must continue to be the same as it was before the game. Cap on but tilted to the left, check. Left sock up, right sock down, check. Shirt out, check. Two pieces of gum in mouth, one in pocket, check. Get on the bus last, check and sit next to . . . oh, no, the things I must do for a successful baseball career.

"That was a good game, Richie," said Chuck. "They were some great hits."

"Thanks."

"Could you show me how to hit like you, Richie? Huh?"

I didn't intend to answer, but that didn't seem to matter. He just kept talking.

"Oh, thanks, Richie. Will you show me how to play right field too? I have trouble catching fly balls."

Fred tapped me on the shoulder and whispered in my ear, "Richie, are you okay? Why don't you tell the nerd to shut up?"

I gave Fred my I'll-tell-you-later look and he sat back in his seat.

"Hey, Richie, could you—" said Chuck.

"Hey, Richie, hey, Richie—" echoed the boys in the back seat.

I couldn't take much more of this but I dared not move. My baseball career was too important.

Why is this ride taking so long?

"Richie, will you teach me how to play shortstop? Oh, forget it, Marty is better than you, I'll ask him."

That's it! I thought. *Career or not, I'm not sitting next to this twerp one minute longer.*

I got up and walked to the back of the van just as the bus pulled into the camp. If I could have just stayed there thirty seconds longer. Maybe I didn't have to stay there until the van got all the way back to camp. Maybe I only had to stay there until the van got to the camp sign. I wasn't sure if the spell had been broken, and I knew I really wouldn't know until we had our next game.

8

"Hey, Fred, will you turn off your flashlight? It's keeping me up."

"Okay, Richie, in a minute."

"What are you doing anyway?"

"Nothing."

I propped myself up on my elbows and stared in the direction of Fred's bunk.

"What are you reading?"

"Oh, nothing."

"Let me see it."

"Go back to sleep and stop asking so many questions," said Fred.

"What are you getting so snippy about?"

"Nothing. Now quiet and let me read."

I lay back down and pretended to go to sleep, but I was really trying to read the title of the book. Fred's fingers covered the first word, but the second word was Pets. *Hmmmm. I never knew Fred was interested in animals. Move your fingers so I can see the rest of the title.* He must have heard my thoughts because a minute later he moved them, and I could see that the first word in the title was Teacher's. *Teacher's Pets,* it sounded like a book about Chuckie. I strained to see the picture on the cover, but it was too dark.

"Teacher's Pets?" I said.

"Shh," said Fred.

"Let me see it."

"Will you go to sleep already?"

"Come on, Fred, be a sport."

"Will you stop bugging me?"

The more Fred told me no, the more I wanted to see the book. He was so engrossed that he didn't see my hand sneaking over. As my fingers reached the front cover, he pulled away, ripping it off.

"You son of a bitch!" he yelled. "You ripped my book."

"I ripped your book?"

"You ripped my book."

"You pulled away."

"Give me my cover back."

"No. I want to look at it. Oh, my God, what kind of a school is this?" There before my eyes were three gorgeous girls sitting on the teacher's desk.

"Girls in my school don't look like this! Where did you get this book?"

"I stole it from my sister. Now give it back."

"Only if you promise to let me read it."

"I'll give it to you after I finish it. The good parts are easy to find. My sister folded over the edge of each page. See, here, read this page."

Fred handed me the book. Hmmm. " 'The teacher slowly pulled down the shades as he . . .' Oh, my God. That's gross! That's disgusting. That's . . . when can I read it?"

"As soon as I'm finished, now give it back to me."

"Okay," I said. "But remember, you promised. My father had a couple of books like that on his night table and so did some of the other people I baby-sit for. When the kids are asleep, I skim through looking for the good parts. One doctor I sat for had all sorts of books on sex, with pictures too."

"I look at my father's *Playboy*s when they go out. He hides them in the bottom drawer of his dresser, but I know where they are. Besides *Playboy,* guess what magazine I like the best?"

"*Penthouse?*"

"No."

"I give up, what?"

"*Sports Illustrated*. Every year around February they have an issue with bathing suits in it and you should see it."

"Oh, yeah, I know which one you mean."

"I've hidden the last two years' issues in my room. My father asked my mother, 'Where's my copy of *Sports Illustrated*?' and she said, 'That's what you get for leaving your things lying around the house. You should be more careful.' My father yelled back, 'I know where things are until you move them.' "

"Hey shut up you guys," yelled Tom and Bill. "We're trying to sleep."

"I'll finish the book in a couple of days and it's yours."

"Don't forget."

"I won't."

"I won't let you."

Two days later I asked Fred if I could have the book, but he got angry and told me not to rush him. I had been thinking about some of the things Fred had read to me the other night and they seemed sort of gross. I couldn't imagine letting a girl see me naked, although I would certainly like to see her. I've known about the facts of life since age eight, but the idea of doing what one is supposed to do with a girl and enjoying it seems yucky. Not me. In fact, I'm not much interested in girls. Well, I sort of am, but I'm not. I like playing baseball or volleyball with them if they are good athletes. I like talking to them sometimes about sports or movies, well maybe only sports, but that's all.

I liked one girl for about a week in seventh grade, but then she got to be a pain. She wanted to walk to class with me and stay on the bus platform with me and talk with me in the hall before school. She used to call me on the phone every night and talk and talk for hours about nothing. I didn't say very much, but even if I wanted to, there wasn't an opportunity. One day her girl friend asked me if I liked her and I said she was okay. The next day her girl friend asked if I liked her very much. I asked if she liked me and she said, "She doesn't like you, she loves you." I was really flattered. "Well, do you like her very much?" she said. "Not very much," I said, "but just okay." When her girl friend told her what I said, I don't think she liked it because she never called me or waited for me in the hall or at the bus again. I really didn't care.

The only other time I was with a girl, sort of, was at our seventh-grade fun night. At the beginning of the year my class had an assembly, like the one for the class trip, and we voted for a dance for one of the fun nights. Now our idea of a dance and the teacher's idea of a dance were quite different. Our class wanted some type of disco dance with a band, lights, the whole thing. Instead we had a square dance with a fat middle-aged lady in a checkered blouse and a ballooned-out dress screeching out instructions over a scratched record. When I heard there was going to be a square dance I wasn't going. My parents said it was fun and Paul was going so I went. The lady had everyone make a circle, boys on the outside and girls on the inside. She played some music and everyone went in opposite directions. When the music stopped, the person that was in front of you was your partner. My partner was at least a head taller than me. When I tried to tell the kid next to me she was his, he refused, so I got stuck. The girl was not only tall, but she was strong too. Whenever the lady said "Swing your partner," she really gave me a SWING! I was afraid that if she ever let go, I would go flying through the air. As soon as the dance was over, I got away from her as fast as I could. Once in a while I would see her in the hall, but I always ducked my head so she wouldn't see me. She was a humungus amazon!

That night, just when we were about to turn out the lights, Fred motioned for me to come over and he gave me the book. He probably knew all along he was going to give it to me tonight, but he just wanted to make me wait. He whispered that I should guard the book, and I had to promise that I would show it to no one else in the bunk. You would think it was a secret CIA document, but I really wanted to read it so I went along with everything. As soon as the lights were out I pulled the covers over my head and turned on my flashlight. I was so involved in the book that when Fred tapped me on the head I let out a scream and threw back the covers. He started to laugh, but I was annoyed.

"What the hell do you want?"

"I just wanted to tell you that the edges of the pages with the good places are turned over."

"I saw that already," I said. "Now let me alone." With that I pulled the covers over my head.

This was probably the dirtiest book I had ever read. Some of the kids in my school had read this book already and asked me if I had. At the time I told them "Sure," and "It was great," but the truth of the matter was, a librarian friend of my mother's told her that I was too young for it, so I was forbidden to read it. Ever since that prohibition I had tried to get a copy. I could feel myself getting tired, but at the same time other parts of my body told me I was also getting excited. I guess my tiredness won because I found the book mashed under me and my flashlight still on the next morning when I woke up. I also found one other thing. Sometime during the night I had had a wet dream. I still feel

sort of embarrassed about them, so I changed into a new pair of underpants before I pushed back the covers and started to get dressed. Not as embarrassed or bewildered, though, as I was the first time I had one. That time was really a nightmare. It really wasn't that long ago; in fact, we had just begun our sex lectures in health class. I can remember the gym teacher standing up in front of the class beside a naked rubber dummy of a man, and he was pointing out the different parts when Paul tapped me on the shoulder and said, "Hey, Richie, my thing was bigger than his when I was two years old." I cracked up and had to put my hands over my mouth to stop, and the teacher gave me a dirty look and said, "Listen up, Mr. Harmon, this is no laughing matter."

Five minutes later, when he turned his back to draw something on the board, Paul tapped me on the shoulder again and said, "Guess what the dummy should sing? 'I wish I had an Oscar Mayer wiener.'" I laughed so hard I fell off my chair. Soon the whole class was singing it.

Everyone had to stay after school that day, and I had to call my mother to come get me. She wanted to know what had happened, but I just told her some kid had acted up and the whole class had to stay.

The next time we had health the gym teacher was five minutes late and one kid had pasted an Oscar Mayer label on the dummy and we were all laughing when he arrived. He threatened to keep the whole class again unless the person who did it confessed. We all stayed again and by this time my mother was getting angry at the gym teacher. She told me she was going to call the school and report him to the principal, but I persuaded her to wait until he did it again. She wanted to know why I was sticking up for the teacher, and I said that he was really a nice guy and I didn't want to see him get into trouble.

My own personal experience with wet dreams came about a month later. One night I suddenly woke up about four o'clock in the morning and felt sort of wet and cold. I think I had been dreaming, but I don't really remember. I tried to fall back to sleep, but the longer I lay there, the wetter and colder it seemed to feel. I reached into my underpants and felt something sticky and that's when I panicked. I turned on the light beside my bed and looked at my fingers. It was very difficult to see because my vision was still blurry, but what I could make out looked a little like Elmer's glue. I threw back the covers and noticed a small stain about the size of a quarter on the front of my underpants and a matching one on the sheet where I had been resting. I slowly pulled the waistband of my underpants to look, when I heard my mother yell, "Richie, are you okay?" *Oh, my God,* I thought, *what if she comes in?*

I quickly let go of the waistband. "I'm fine, Mom, I just had to blow my nose."

"You're not sick?"

She knows. I know she knows. She'll be in here soon. I'm doomed.

"No, Mom, really I'm fine."

I decided I had to see what was going on so I got out of bed and went into the bathroom. I looked inside my underwear. Maybe there was something wrong with my penis, like it was injured. I looked at it, but it didn't seem swollen and it didn't hurt when I touched it. I tried to go to the bathroom. No luck. I turned on the water. Still no luck. *Oh, my God. What do you do if your penis is broken? What happens to the pee?*

Thank God I didn't have to wait for an answer to the question because I began to go. Now I was more puzzled than ever.

Maybe I have some horrible disease. Oh, no, I'm going to die. Maybe I'm dying right now. I'd better clean up the mess in my bed and get my dirty underpants in the hamper because I don't know how long I'm going to last.

I quickly cleaned things up and got back in bed.

What if I don't last until morning?

I jumped out of bed and found a crayon and a piece of paper. "Dear Mom, Dad, Robby, and Sally . . ." I began. Then it hit me. I remembered the sex lectures and the talk about wet dreams. I really wasn't paying much attention when the gym teacher talked about them, but now I wished I had. I knew one thing for sure, I wasn't going to die. I got back into bed. Then I went to sleep.

I can smile now when I think about that night. But then, it wasn't funny.

"Hey, Richie," said Fred, "looks like you enjoyed the book last night."

I looked down. I guess I had.

* * *

I try to avoid my brother and sister as much as possible. They're such pains. But the other day when I was leaving the dining room after lunch, Robby spotted me and before I could get away he yelled.

"Hey, Richie, Mommy told me to show you this letter," Robby said. I took it.

> Dear Robby,
>
> How are you? We are all fine. Last weekend we visited Aunt Edna at the shore. The weather was very hot. I can't wait to see you on visiting day. Send me a list of things you want. We have only gotten three letters from your brother. Please show him this letter and tell him to write.
>
> Love and Kisses,
> Mommy and Daddy

"Don't forget to write, Richie."

"I have written."

"But the letter says—"

"I can read."

"Hey, Richie, what's this I hear that you got into a fight with one of your bunkmates."

"It was nothing."

"What happened?"

"You know that tall guy, Jimmy, the one with the curly hair? Well, he called me a jerk, so I popped him one."

"Good for you."

"That kid's got potential," I thought.

"Well, see ya later. Don't forget to write."

"I told you I would."

"Well, don't forget."

Just when I think Robby's getting to be like one of the guys, he spoils it by acting like my brother. I really hate to write letters. There is nothing interesting to say.

Out of the corner of my eye I caught a glimpse of a familiar little dumpy shape leaving the dining hall. It was my sister. Maybe if I just stood still, she wouldn't recognize me. "Just be cool, don't breathe. She's probably halfway up to the bunk by now. You've made it home free. Deep breath."

"Hey, Richie, Mommy told me to give you this letter."

"Forget it, Sally. I know what it says."

If she tells me to write, I'll kill her. I can see the headlines: ANGRY BROTHER KILLS SISTER.

Dear Mom and Dad. How are you? I am fine. I killed Sally yesterday. Love, Richie.

"Well, then, Richie . . ."

"Don't say it, Sally. I'm gonna write. I promise I'll do it."

"Richie, how long until visiting day?"

"Another week, Sally. It will pass fast, you'll see."

"I really miss Mommy and Daddy."

"Listen, Sally, I have to go and write Mom and Dad a letter."

"So long, Richie."

"See ya, Sally."

"What am I gonna write?" I thought, as I walked back to the bunk. I got out a postcard and addressed it. "What will I . . . I've got it."

"Dear Mom and Dad." The rest of the card I left blank. In the bottom left-hand corner I wrote, "This letter has been written in invisible ink. Put over a flame to get message."

Now for more important things.

9

"Are you going to ask a girl to go out with you to-night in a boat?" asked Fred.

"If they're lucky," I said. "How about you?"

"I don't know yet."

"I know someone who would be perfect for you, Fred."

"Who?"

"Carolyn," I said seriously.

"Carolyn," yelled Fred. "You mean Moby Blumenthal? The boat would probably sink. Someone would have to take her out in a barge."

"She's got a good personality."

"All fat girls have good personalities. God had to give them something."

"How about Amy?"

"Amy?"

"The cute one with the short brown hair."

"Na, she's not my type."

"I think she's really cute. Maybe I'll ask her out. Hey, maybe she has a cute girl friend for you so we could go out in the boat together."

"Hey, that's a great idea. At least we'll have each other to talk to if the girls turn out to be duds. What are you going to wear?"

"I don't know. What are you going to wear?"

"I don't know."

"Do you think this shirt goes with these jeans?"

"I don't know."

"How about these sneakers and this belt?"

"I don't know."

"What do you know?"

"I don't know."

"You are really a big help," I said. You might think I was asking for something complicated. I just couldn't decide for myself. *Should I wear the*

jeans and a T-shirt or the khakis and a sweat shirt?
They both looked good. *I wish my mom were here;
she would know what to pick. Oh, my God, I hope
nobody heard me think that! I'd be laughed right
out of the bunk. Strike out that last thought! I know
how to decide. Eaney, meaney, mighty, moe and
out goes y-o-u, the jeans win so I will pick this one,
the khakis win unless I decide to pick the other,
jeans, and this could go on all night, khakis, I must
pick this one, jeans, now khakis, finally jeans.*

"Richie, why are you staring at your clothes?"

"What's that, Fred?"

"Why are you staring at your clothes?"

"I wasn't staring at my clothes."

"I just saw you staring at your clothes, moving
your hand back and forth."

"What are you talking about?"

"Forget it. You only have five minutes to get
dressed, and if you're not ready, I'm not waiting."

"So leave, see if I care."

I really did care but I didn't like the way Fred was
getting on my case. *Why is he bugging me so much
about staring? I wasn't staring.* I picked up my jeans

75

and pulled them on quickly. *Let's see now, do I want to smell herbal or unscented? Should I have the wet look or the dry look? Maybe I'll use what Joe Namath uses. No, that Ralph Lauren stuff is nice, or maybe I'll mix the two and come up with an aroma of my own. Richie, the smell of distinction. It makes a twelve-year-old boy smell like a . . . I don't want to smell. I'm not going to use anything.* The T-shirt and sneakers followed, and I was just putting the final touches on my hair when everyone was ready to leave. I lagged a little behind the group because I didn't want Fred to think he could boss me around. I wondered what was bugging Fred today. I really couldn't come up with anything. When I arrived at the lake, the first thing I did was to get some food and find a spot where I could eat and look over the girls.

"Mind if I join you?" asked Fred.

"No, sit down, the view is great from here." I hoped he wouldn't continue to act obnoxious.

"Hey, Fred, check out the girl over there next to Amy."

"The skinny one?"

"Skinny? She is not skinny!"

"You don't think that girl in the brown shorts is skinny?"

"How would you like being with her tonight?"

"Na, she's not my type."

"Why not?"

"I don't know."

"Well, how do you know if she's not your type?"

"I don't know, I just know."

"Okay, okay, how about the girl next to her?"

"She's ugly."

"Ugly?"

"Yeah, she looks like the Clearasil poster girl."

"Okay then, who do you like?"

"I don't know. Listen, Richie, I have a good idea. How about if you ask Amy if she has any cute girl friends for me and that's who I'll go out with?"

"Why don't you ask Amy yourself?"

"Why should I ask her if she's your girl friend?"

"My girl friend? I've never talked to her, besides you're the one that wants to go out with her girl friend, not me."

"What's the matter, Richie, afraid to ask?"

"Me afraid, that's a laugh. I don't see you running over to ask."

"I'd ask for you if it were my girl friend, and besides, I'm still hungry and I want another hamburger."

"I want another one too and maybe a piece of corn."

"Okay, Richie, let's flip a coin. One flip, the loser has to ask. Okay?"

"Okay. Call it in the air. Heads."

"Tails! Richie, you ask."

"Let me see that. You cheated."

"What's fair is fair unless, of course, you're chicken."

"Who are you calling chicken, Fred? I ain't no chicken. But first I still want that other hamburger."

Now let's see, what should I say? "Hi! My name is Richie, what's yours?" No, too corny. "Hi! My name is Richie, can you row a boat?" Ycchhh. "Hi! My name is Richard. Since this is your first year here at camp, how would you like to take a moonlit tour of the camp by boat with me?" Hey, that sounds great. I can hear it all now. "Oh, Richie, that would be wonderful" "By the way, if you have a girl friend who is as sensational-looking as you, who would like to go out with another good-looking guy, we could go out double" "Michelle would be perfect." "Michelle?" "Yes, the tall blonde over there by the—"

"Richie, are you done with your hamburger yet?"

"What?"

"Are you going to ask her today?"

"Sure, Fred, sure, just don't rush me."

"The thing will be over before you decide."

"I'm going. I'm going."

As I walked toward Amy, I practiced what I was going to say. *Hello, my name is Richard. Since this is your first year . . .* There was no more time to practice. There I was standing in front of Amy and two other girls. She looked up and my mind went blank. My tongue felt fat and heavy. Beads of sweat formed on my forehead and I wondered if my protection was still working. Then the letters *H* and *I* came to me and in a flash I blurted out, "Hi!" Amy seemed startled at first by the outburst, but she didn't let it stop her from replying, "Hi!" "My name is Richard" appeared in my mind, and as it did, I said, "My name is Richie." "Hi, Richie, my name is Amy."

79

"Hi, Amy, my name is Richie." It came out again and I felt a little embarrassed. Amy giggled a little. "I know, you just said that." "Listen, Amy, how would you like to go out for a boat ride with me tonight?" Without any hesitation she said, "Sure."

"Richie, would you mind if we went out with somebody else?"

"Mind, I think that is a great idea."

"Great, I have a girl friend who I'm dying to fix up with my cousin."

"Your cousin?"

"Yes, my cousin is in your bunk."

"He is? What's his name?"

"Chuck."

I couldn't believe what I was hearing. This must be a dream, no a nightmare. I wanted to roll the clock back two and a half hours and start over again.

"Chuck is your cousin?"

"Look, there he is over there. Chuck, come over here. I want to introduce you to someone."

"Chuck is your cousin? Chuck is your cousin?" I repeated.

Chuck was coming toward us now. I looked over at Fred, hoping he would get me out of this, but a puzzled look appeared on his face, and he motioned, "What the hell is going on?"

"Hi, Cous, hi, Richie, what's doin'?"

"Hi, Chuckie. How would you like to join Richie and me and my girl friend Marsha for a ride on the lake?"

"No thanks, Amy. I might get sick in the boat."

"In that case," I said quickly, "maybe you'd better stay here. I wouldn't want you to be sick."

"Oh, Chuckie, don't be a party pooper, you won't get sick."

"The water looks a little rough tonight," I said, "maybe you'd better sit this one out."

"Don't listen to him. Look at how calm and peaceful the lake looks. Come on, let me introduce you to Marsha and then we can pick out a boat. Marsha, this is my cousin Chuckie. Chuckie, this is my girl friend Marsha. Marsha, Richie. Richie, Marsha."

"You pick out a boat. I'll be right there," I said, as I walked over in Fred's direction.

"What's happening, Richie? What girl did I get?"

"Fred, you are not going to believe this, but Amy is Chuckie's cousin."

"His what?"

"His cousin, and I'm going to be in a boat with Chuck soon if you can't help me come up with some excuse fast."

"Tell him you broke your arm and you can't row."

"They won't believe that."

"Tell them you have food poisoning. There was a tapeworm in the corn."

"Be serious."

"Richie, hurry up. We're waiting for you," yelled Amy, Marsha, and Chuck in unison.

"Fred, help me!"

"Richie, hurry up."

"Fred!"

"Richie!" they yelled.

Doomed.

"I'm coming," I yelled in disgust. I glanced back at Fred. He had a smirk on his face, and I wanted to run back and relocate his nose. *Ask me to help you out sometime,* I thought. *I'll help you just like you helped me.*

How do I get myself into these things? I feel like the comic-strip character that walks around with a black cloud over his head. I didn't want to ruin things between Amy and myself, so I managed to force a smile on my face by the time I got to the boat. Chuck and Marsha were already sitting in the back of the boat, and Amy was waiting for me on the dock.

"You row first, and later when Chuckie rows, you and I can sit in the back together."

This girl really has good ideas, I thought. *It's not her fault that Chuck is her cousin.* In fact, I really didn't mind rowing because it would give me a chance to show Amy my muscles.

Things didn't start out that bad. Marsha was asking Chuck some questions about himself and he was responding with dumb answers, but I expected that. For some unknown reason it was much easier for me to talk to Amy, and I was even able to come up with some good lines that made her laugh out loud. Then Chuck interrupted me to say he had a nose bleed. Why and how it happened, I don't know.

"Oh, my God!" he yelled. "My nose is bleeding!" And he began to jump up and down, and by the way he was acting, you might think he was hemorrhaging to death and had only a few minutes to live.

"What should I do? It won't stop."

"Somebody do something quick," screamed Amy.

Just what I needed. A hysterical girl to go along with a bleeding weirdo.

Calmly I told him to sit down and put his head back.

"If I lean back, I'll fall out of the boat."

What a perfect solution, I thought.

"No, Chuck, listen. Put your head on Marsha's lap and press on either side of the bridge of your nose with your thumb and index finger."

Chuck had hardly put his head down, when he popped up.

"The blood is running down in my throat and it tastes horrible."

"Oh, Chuckie, are you all right?" said Amy.

"It's making me sick," he moaned.

"Be calm," I said calmly.

"I'm going to throw up."

"If you throw up, so will I," said Marsha.

"I can feel it coming."

"Richie, do something," shouted Amy.

"If you throw up, so will I," shouted Marsha again.

"I can feel it coming," screamed Chuck.

"Everyone be calm," I yelled. "God damn it! Everyone shut up and listen. Now, Chuck, you change seats with Amy. That way if you throw up, you can do it by yourself over the end of the boat. In the meantime take deep breaths."

"I can feel it coming," he said. "I'm afraid to move. I'll fall in."

That's what I figured. He can't breathe and walk at the same time, I thought.

"Keep breathing deeply and give me your hand."

"Oh, Chuckie, be careful," Amy yelled in my ear.

"If you throw up, so will I," said Marsha.

I started to lead Chuck past me. He stopped, his face turning a pale green.

"It's coming now, Richie. I can't stop it."

"Breathe deeply," I yelled.

"It's com—" And with that Chuck rushed to the side of the boat where I was standing. His sudden movement surprised me, and as he brushed by, I lost my balance and fell backward into the cold muddy water. I scrambled to the surface, only to come face to face with Chuck hanging over the side vomiting.

"Chuckie, are you all right?" said Amy.

"If you throw up, so will I," said Marsha.

No one seemed to be the least bit concerned that I had fallen overboard and was probably getting barfed on.

I pulled myself up over the side and flopped into the boat. Amy and Marsha moaned.

Chuckie had stopped vomiting and was now sitting on the floor in the front of the boat.

"Richie, are you okay? I didn't mean to knock you in."

Hooray, at least someone recognizes that I fell into the water.

I sat down and started to row toward shore.

"Hey, Richie, where are you going now?"

I didn't answer.

"My nose has stopped bleeding and I don't feel sick anymore," Chuck said. "When can I have my time to row?"

I didn't answer. My teeth were beginning to chatter.

Marsha and Amy were now laughing and giggling. It was as if nothing had happened.

"Why are we heading toward shore?" asked Amy.

"It's still early," said Chuck.

"I don't feel sick anymore," said Marsha.

I looked first at the girls and then back at Chuck. I knew then why some people are driven to murder others. I didn't answer, but I quickened my rowing pace.

"Richie is a spoilsport," said Amy, and Marsha and Chuck chimed in, "Richie is a spoilsport!"

If I'm a spoilsport, then you are . . . I couldn't think of a word dirty enough to express my feelings.

When I got to shore, I jumped out of the boat, leaving Chuck and the girls still sitting there. I ran as fast as I could in the direction of the bunk. As I passed Fred he called out, "How come you came back so early?"

I didn't want to talk to anyone so I ignored Fred and kept running. The first thing I did when I got back to the bunk was to dump Chuck's bed and cubby. I wanted to dump all the beds and cubbies. I got out of my wet clothes and threw them in a pile.

Those girls were as weird as Chuck. That's it for me and girls. I went in and took a hot shower.

10

Revenge. Someday, somehow, I would get my revenge against cousin Chuckie. All sorts of fiendish plans passed through my mind as I lay in bed that night. Toothpaste in his bed. Not messy enough. Toothpaste and lake water. Still not messy enough. Toothpaste, lake water, and horse manure. Sounded like a great combination, but somehow I wanted something more devastating. Maybe I'd find a reason to pick a fight and then I could beat the crap out of him. Pow! To the face. Smash! Pow! To the nose. Blood begins to flow. Jab! Jab! To the eye. Another Pow! Smash! To the nose. Two kerpows to the stomach. He's down. Eight, nine, ten. So what! So you can beat up a nerd. That just makes you a turkey beater-upper. Nothing more, nothing less. What I needed was something that was clever but sneaky. I fell asleep unsatisfied, still without a plan.

Sometime during the night I had a very weird dream. I was on a deserted island with Chuck. I don't know how long I had been there, but it had been long enough for me to be completely fed up with him. I guess I had chased him around the island and caught him. All I remember was seeing him lying spread-eagle, each leg tied to a bent-over tree. I walked over and cut the ropes that tied down the trees, and as they sprang back, Chuck was ripped in half and thrown a hundred feet into the air. I smiled, thinking I had finally rid myself of him, but when his body finally landed, there were two of them. They began to chase me. I ran as fast as I could until I came to a cliff and then I jumped. Next thing I knew I was on the floor next to my bed. I must have awakened Fred for he rolled over and cursed at me and went back to sleep. I got up and on my way to the bathroom I thought of strangling Chuck. I could feel my muscles tensing and my fingers curving to the shape of his neck. I could see it all now: THIRTEEN-

YEAR-OLD BOY GETS LIFE FOR MURDERING BUNK-
MATE. PARENTS WAIL AS BOY THROWS HIMSELF
ON THE MERCY OF THE COURT. *"He was a good
boy,"* said Mrs. Finster, his kindergarten teacher. *"I
remember when he used to come into my grocery
store and ask for candy,"* said Mr. Whiter. *"I never
knew my brother was a homicidal maniac,"* re-
marked his brother. *"I knew he was,"* said his sister.

My fingers opened and my muscles relaxed. *I'm
innocent. I didn't do it. I didn't do it. I'm too young
to die,* I thought. So I went to the bathroom and
then went back to sleep.

The next day, instead of going to breakfast, I
went up to the ball field and sat by myself on the
bleachers. I didn't want to face anyone, at least not
yet. The water clogging my right ear reminded me of
last night. I lay back and closed my eyes. The peace
and quiet was nice. It felt good to be alone.

"Hey, Richie, I've been looking all over for you.
Are you okay?" I sat up with a start. It was my
brother.

"Okay? What are you talking about?"

"It's all over camp."

"What's all over camp?"

"How you drowned last night and how Chuck jumped into the lake and saved you."

"What? Who told you that?"

"It's all over camp."

"I'm going to kill him."

"Who?"

"Chuck."

"But he saved your life. Why would you want to kill him?"

"I don't want to talk about it."

"What?"

"Just leave me alone."

After Robby left, I lay down again and I guess I fell asleep. I probably would have slept all morning if it weren't for:

"Were there really crocodiles and snakes?"

"Crocodiles and what?" I said, sitting up. It was my sister.

"Robby told me you were here."

Good old Robby. Go away, Sally.

"Were there really crocodiles and snakes?"

"Sally, I don't want to talk about it."

"Boy, that Chuck was sure brave."

"Sally . . ."

"What a man!"

I raised my fist and Sally started to run. I didn't bother to chase her. I was too mad.

Visiting day marked the midpoint of the camping season. It also marked the third consecutive year our bunk held the guess-how-many-Cadillacs-will-be-here-today pool. For fifty cents you could write down your number. The closest one got all the money. I was hot off winning last year and I wanted to make it two in a row.

The second important thing about visiting day was all the food the parents brought. Everyone in the bunk asked their parents to bring up tons of food because the night after they left, we had our annual all-night-stuff-your-face-pig-out party. Last year we even gave out awards for the Best Home-made Dessert, Cake Category. Fred's mom won with her banana chocolate layer cake. Best Homemade Dessert, Cookie Category. My mother won with her chewy extra-delicious chocolate chip raisin cookies. Best Cold Cuts. Four neighborhood delica-tessens were nominated and I think the one from New York won. Other categories included Most Amount of Food, Most Candy, Best Assortment of

Candy, Most Healthful Assortment of Nonadditive or Nonpreservative Natural Nutritious Food, Least Candy, Most Original Food Item. One parent brought up a cold pizza with everything on it. I never had cold pizza before, and except for the cold ground meat, it didn't taste that bad. And finally, Most Embarrassing Food Item. Last year John got a glass doggy filled with prunes.

The third and last thing about visiting day was I got to see my parents. I don't like to admit it, and I would surely deny saying it if anyone quoted me, but after four weeks of being away I think I missed them a little. Not very much, mind you, only a little. If you were to ask me why, I really couldn't tell you for sure. I certainly didn't miss the "clean up your room," or "take a shower," or "turn off the TV right now and do your homework." What did I miss? I don't know for sure.

Visiting day itself was always on a Sunday, but the camp began to prepare for it a couple days before. When I say prepare for it, I don't mean anything out in the open; I mean something subtle so that most of the kids don't know that it's happening. For instance, my brother and sister both had complained bitterly about how mean their counselors were, but now they told me that their counselor had been very nice for the past two days.

I also noticed that the food had changed. Saturday lunch was fresh hot turkey sandwiches. Saturday dinner was steak and Sunday breakfast was eggs and pancakes, not just one or the other. And Saturday night after evening activity, guess what? That's right. A surprise ice cream night!

I really never thought much about these things, but now I did and it made me angry. I didn't stay angry very long, though, because the excitement of Sunday built up throughout the week. Even though visiting day was not scheduled to start until ten thirty, parents started to come around ten A.M.

I stood near the road that ran along the outside of camp with Fred and two other guys in my bunk, and we watched the trickle of cars slowly become a heavy snakelike stream. Fred was the first to spot his parents and he bounded off toward their car. Then Marty and John saw their parents and I was left to wait by myself. I felt a little mad since I had told my parents that everyone comes about ten A.M. and they should too. *"If the owners wanted us to come at ten* A.M., they would say so in the letter," my mother would reply. "Don't you believe me when I tell you that everyone comes at ten A.M. except you?" "It's not that I don't believe you, but we don't want to break the rules of camp," said my father. "If you don't want to break rules, then why did you drive so fast last March that you got a speeding ticket, and then why did you ask Uncle Art to see if he could fix the ticket up for you?" I thought, but didn't say.

Damn it! If they don't get here soon, Robby and Sally will be very upset, and I don't want that to happen. Wait! Is that their car? It is, they're here. Boy I can't wait to tell them—ohhh, it's not their car. Where are they? I hope that . . . There they are. It looks like they have other people with them. Oh, no, they came up with Chuck's parents. How could they do that to me? If I know them, they'll want to do everything with his parents and I'll have to be with that creep all afternoon and that will ruin my . . . Hey wait! That wasn't their car.

"Hey, Richie," Robby called.

I knew he'd be upset. How was I going to calm him down?

"Richie! Richie, where've you been, I've been looking all over for you. Mom and Dad have been here for fifteen minutes. Come on, they're up by my bunk."

"How could I have missed them? I saw every single car that came in. Oh, well, did Mom and Dad bring up a package for me?" I asked as we walked.

"I didn't see any," he said.

"Come on, Robby, tell me the truth, did they?"

"I am telling the truth!"

"No, really, don't kid, this is serious."

"I am serious."

"I'll punch you in the face if there is a package."

"Go ahead and try it. I ain't afraid of you!"

"Yeah, come over here and say that."

"Richie, Robby, how many times have I told you to be nice to each other?" my mother called from the steps of the bunk.

"I am nice to him. He started it."

"I did not start it, Richie started it."

"Boys, please. Can't you stop fighting long enough to say hello?" she said.

"Oh, yeah, hi, Mom, hi, Dad. Did you bring the food?"

"Can't you even come over and give me a little hug?" said my mother.

I hugged her. "Now can we get the packages?"

"There are packages for each of you in the car," said my mother.

"See, I told you they brought them!"

"I never said they didn't bring them, Richie!"

"Boys, please," pleaded my mother. "If you don't stop, I'll slowly get a headache."

My mother didn't have to say any more. I realized that her medical fate lay in my hands. Of all the weapons that parents have, like threats of taking something away, physical punishment, or banishment to your room, the scariest one is the thought of causing your parents some physical problem: "If you don't stop, you will give your father high blood pressure," or "See, your fighting caused your mother to get chest pain." It works every time.

We left the packages in our bunks, and my father went off with Robby and me while my mother spent the morning with Sally. At noon we met and had a picnic lunch, and my mother took my sister and me

99

and my father took Robby. At three o'clock we met again, and I had a chance to be alone with my father.

I had been looking forward to this all afternoon because I had so much to tell him about camp. I also wanted to ask him for advice about Chuck.

"Did you ever hate somebody so much that you wanted to get revenge?"

After the question came out, I was sorry I had asked it. I could predict what he'd say: "You know, Richie, it's not nice to hate someone that much," or "You know, Richie, two wrongs don't make a right," and I guess I really couldn't blame him. Parents are supposed to set good examples and teach children right from wrong. I'll probably do the same thing with my kids if I ever get married and have a family.

It seemed as if my father was taking a very long time to answer the question, so I thought, one, he didn't hear the question and he was waiting for me to repeat it, two, he was preparing an extra-long talk on brotherhood, friendship, and the American way of life, or three, the question was too difficult for him. If the reason was one, then I could ask him another question and he would never know. If it was two, I could ask another question, hoping to save myself from the lecture, and if it was three, he would welcome another question because it would get him off the hook.

Just as I opened my mouth, my father said, "The school I went to was so small it only had one class for each grade, so we went from kindergarten up through eighth grade with the same group of kids. There was one kid named Danny who bullied everyone, and over the years I grew to hate him intensely. By sixth grade I felt confident and strong enough to fight him and beat him, but somehow that solution didn't seem good enough. I wanted to get him in a way he wouldn't forget. One day a great idea came to me. Halloween was coming up and I knew just how to scare the hell out of him. I began to drop stories about the one-armed hobo who attacked boys on Halloween night. I let a couple of other kids in on my plan, and whenever they heard my stories, they agreed and added stories of their own. By Halloween night Danny almost seemed convinced that there really was a hobo but he told everyone that if he met up with that hobo guy, he'd set him straight.

"That night I dressed up like the one-armed hobo

and hid in the bushes two houses from Danny's. When he came by, I leaped out at him and started to growl. He let out a scream and ran full speed toward his house, dropping his Halloween candy on the way. The next day he wasn't in school, but when he returned, he seemed a little bit more subdued."

I don't know why, but the story surprised me. It's funny, but I never really think of my pop as a kid doing kid's things. I've heard him tell stories about what his parents did to him when he was a kid, but never anything quite like this.

"Thanks, Dad," I said with a smile.

"For what?"

"For giving me a great idea."

"Walter, Walter." I could hear my mother's melodious voice. "It's time to leave."

I was really never big on long good-byes, so I gave my mother a quick hug, shook my father's hand, and started back to the bunk.

"Don't forget to write," he said.

"I won't," I yelled back.

"Take care of your brother and sister," my mom called.

"I will."

Just as it started to pull away, I ran back to the car. I tapped on the side window and my father rolled it down.

"Thanks again, Dad," I said. "Thanks."

I didn't wait for a reply, but turned and ran as fast as I could back to the bunk.

11

"Hey, Richie," yelled Fred as he burst into the bunk, "the oldest girls just had their camp-out night changed to next week."

"So."

"So we get to go in their place this Friday."

"The one-armed hobo."

"The one-armed hobo? Have you flipped your lid?"

"It's perfect."

"What's perfect?"

"Fred, I'll need your help."

"Richie, what are you talking about?"

"Shh, quiet, Fred. I have a plan to scare the crap out of Chuck. Do you want to help?"

"Do I?"

"Okay, shh, listen. We'll need at least two other guys . . ."

For the rest of that day and the remaining four days before the camp-out, Fred, Marty, John, and I told Chuck stories about the one-armed hobo.

"He only attacks at night," I told him.

"He seems to go after short boys with glasses," Fred told him.

"For some reason he seems to hate boys who get bloody noses and vomit," John told him.

At first Chuck laughed, but after a couple of days he finally went to Mike, who said we were just kidding. Mike told us to knock it off. At that point I decided we had done enough to set the stage.

After lunch on Friday our bunk piled into the camp van. The campsite was thirty miles away. I sat next to Chuck and told him not to worry because I would sleep with him in his tent to protect him from the one-armed hobo.

"Cut it out, Richie," he said. "Mike says there is

no such thing as the one-armed hobo, and if you don't stop it, I'm going to tell Mike you're still bothering me."

"Okay, okay," I said, "I was just trying to help."

"No, you're not. I know you. You are trying to upset me."

"Okay, okay, forget I said anything."

"Don't be mad at me, Richie. I still want you to sleep with me."

"I'm not mad at you. Sure I'll sleep with you."

"Boy, this is working out perfectly," I thought. "I can't wait till nighttime when Fred comes into our tent posing as the one-armed hobo. I'll act a little scared just for effect, but Chuck—he'll probably get up and scream and run around and I'll enjoy every minute of it."

Nighttime couldn't come fast enough. After dinner I pulled Fred aside and asked him if he knew exactly what to do. He was a little annoyed with me because it was the fifth time since we got there that I had asked him if he knew exactly what to do. I promised him I wouldn't ask again, but he just looked at me with a you-said-that-before-but-still-ask-me-again look.

As it started to get dark, we all sat around the fire roasting marshmallows and singing songs. Mike asked us if we wanted to hear a story. "Yes," we yelled.

"This is a true story," he began. "In fact, it happened four years ago today. I wasn't at camp that year and a group of my friends at home decided to have a picnic. We all piled into a van and drove about fifteen miles till we found a nice spot near a deserted farmhouse. Well, everything was going along just fine, until all of a sudden, you guessed it, it started to rain. Since it was only two o'clock, we didn't want to go home so we went to the deserted farmhouse, which was dry and relatively clean, and we spread out our food and blanket and continued our picnic. Around seven thirty it started to get dark, but we still didn't want to leave so we tried the lights. They didn't work, so Bill found a candle and lit it and went down into the basement to check the fuse box. We were having such a good time we didn't notice how long he had been away, but when we did, we all became a little apprehensive."

Mike paused here and the expression on his face

got a little grim. All of us shifted a bit. I must tell you truthfully, I wasn't scared at all.

"Well," said Mike, continuing, "no one wanted to go down into the basement alone. So the rest of us all decided to go down together. When we finally got to the basement door, we found Bill's candle lying on its side still smoking. We lit the candle again and proceeded slowly down the steps. On the second step we found Bill's left arm. The girls screamed and I choked in terror. His right arm was on the fourth step and his legs were lying in a heap at the bottom of the steps. We held each other's hands tightly as we approached the fuse box. There, beneath it, was Bill's head with a big broad smile on it and blood dripping from his lips."

Mike paused again as the guys gasped. I knew this was a put-on, but I gasped too just to be part of the group. Mike went on, looking everyone straight in the eye.

"The sight was horrible. More horrible than you can imagine, but it must have been too much for John, one of the guys in the group, for he started yelling and screaming and nothing we did could calm him down. The next day he was committed to a mental hospital and he is there to this day. You know, it's a funny thing, every year on the anniversary of that horrible happening, one of the remaining members of the group remembers that incident and the memory is just too much, for it drives him crazy."

Mike paused again. A long silence. Then he began to run wildly around toward us, yelling "And now it's my turn to go crazy! And now it's my turn to go crazy!"

I ran away just like the others when he came toward me, but I'm not lying, I wasn't scared at all. After all the guys finally calmed down Mike told us that it was bedtime. I winked at Fred and he winked back at me just as I disappeared with Chuck in the tent.

"Boy, I hope I can sleep after that story," said Chuck.

"Sure you'll be able to sleep. What could happen?"

"That one-armed hobo stuff was just a joke, wasn't it?"

"Sure, Chuck, sure. We can't fool you, you're too smart for us."

"I knew it all the time, Richie. I knew it all the time."

"Go to sleep now, Chuck, I'm tired."

"Okay, Richie, good night."

About five minutes later I heard something scratching and moaning outside the tent. I had to hold myself back from laughing out loud.

"Hey, Richie, what's that?"

"Go to sleep, Chuck, I didn't hear anything."

"No, Richie, listen."

There was silence.

"What are you talking about?"

"I don't hear it anymore either. I guess I'm just jumpy."

"Go to sleep."

Now we heard more scratching, moaning, and howling.

Chuck jumped up and yelled, "There it is, Richie. You hear that, don't you?"

"Sure I hear that, but it's probably some animal."

"It's not an animal, it's . . ."

"Oh, Chuck, go to bed, it's nothing."

Boy, I thought to myself, *Fred should get an Academy Award. This is great.*

"Okay, Richie, I'll go to sleep."

Just as Chuck put his head down, a low voice began to speak, "I am the one-armed hobo and I'm out to get you."

"Richie, it's the one-armed hobo!" yelled Chuck.

"Yes, it's the one-armed hobo and I'm out to get you. Here I come!"

Chuck didn't wait to see what entered the tent as he ripped up one of the sides and ran out into the night.

I was laughing so hard at what happened, I almost didn't hear the voice continuing to talk.

"I'm the one-armed hobo and I'm out to get you!"

When I finally got a hold of myself, I called out for Fred to stop.

"I'm the one-armed hobo and I'm out to get you. You cannot escape."

"Okay, Fred, enough, you were great."

"No one can stop me. Haaa haaa haaa."

"Bravo, Fred. Great!" And I started to applaud.

"I am the one-armed hobo!"

"Okay, Fred, don't overdo it."

"And I'm out to get you."

"Okay, Fred, I know what you want, you want me to come out and shake your hand."

"I am out to get you."

When I pulled back the flap of the tent and went outside, there was no one there.

"Fred!" I yelled. There was silence. "Fred, where are you? Come on, Fred, don't play around like this. It ain't funny." Silence. "Fred? Fred? Where are you?"

I ran over to Fred's tent and ripped open the flap. Fred was pretending to be asleep.

"Okay, Fred, I know you are faking. Wake up!" Fred was silent.

"Come on, Fred. Enough is enough. Get up!"

And with that I shook him vigorously.

He awoke with a start. "Richie, oh, my God, you scared me!"

"Come on, Fred, you were great."

"I'm sorry, Richie, I guess I fell asleep. Is it too late to scare Chuck?"

"Too late? You just did scare Chuck."

I imitated how he sounded: "I am the one-armed hobo and I'm out to get you."

"Richie, honest, I fell asleep. I'm sorry."

"You were sleeping?"

"Yes."

"Well, if it wasn't you, who was it?"

"I don't know, but I don't like this at all. This is really getting creepy."

"You're scared, my teeth are about to fly out of my mouth."

"Listen, Richie, there must be some logical explanation."

"But what is it?"

"Calm down. Let me think."

"I am calm, you're the one that's upset, not me."

"I'm not upset, you are."

"Of course," I said calmly, "I know what happened. John probably did it. Remember when we were setting up the whole thing, he said he wanted to do it and you said you wanted to do it, and remember how John said he was going to do it anyway?"

"Yeah, John did it," said Fred. "Let's go to his tent and tell him how great he was."

So Fred and I went to John's tent, but he was sound asleep too. When we woke him up, he denied doing anything. So now there were three of us who were sort of scared. I guess our talking woke up the rest of the guys because everyone seemed to be coming out of their tents and asking what was happening. I told them about the one-armed hobo trick and we didn't know what to think. We all decided it was time to tell Mike. Just as we were about to open his flap we heard growling noises behind us. We all turned around to see the silhouette of a one-armed man standing in the bushes about fifty feet away.

"I'm the one-armed hobo," he bellowed, "and I am out to get you." With that he ran toward us.

I started to run toward the woods, but my feet tangled with Fred's and we fell over one another. Before I had a chance to get up, the one-armed man was upon me and he grabbed the collar of my sweat shirt and began to twist it.

Oh, my God. I'm too young to die.

"Fred, John, help, someone please!" But everyone had scattered. My only chance was to wake up Mike. So at the top of my lungs I yelled, "MIKE!

MIKE! HELP ME! PLEASE! MIKE, ANSWER ME. MIKE, HELP! I'M BEING KILLED."

The one-armed man tightened his grip and said in a booming voice, "I won't kill you if you promise never to tease Chuck again."

"I promise, I promise!" I said.

The man loosened his grip and began to laugh. At first I was confused, but then I recognized the laugh. It was Mike.

"I knew it was you all the time," I said. "You didn't fool me."

Mike didn't say anything more to me, but he yelled for all the guys to get back in their tents and go to sleep and then he disappeared into his. I went back into my tent, where I found Chuck sound asleep. He must have known all the time. I promised never to tease him, but I didn't promise never to kill him. Let's see, should I use a gun or a knife? . . . But I was too tired to think. I fell asleep.

The next morning I was sitting outside my tent pretending to gaze at nature. That's what I wanted everyone else to think, but that really wasn't what I was concentrating on. Right then there was a war going on inside my head.

I'm angry as hell at Mike for messing up things last night, and I don't want him to be angry at me for teasing Chuck. It was only a joke. What's wrong with a good joke? Chuck would have been so scared, but no, Mike had to stick his two cents in. Honest, Mike, I didn't mean any harm; besides it was none of your business. Oh, I get it now, I'm not allowed to tease or scare anybody, but you can tease or scare. I wasn't that scared anyway. Right? Wrong. No way.

"Is there something wrong, Richie?"

Mike's question startled me since I didn't hear him coming.

"Huh?" I said.

"You look like something is wrong."

I stared Mike straight in the eye. *He's angry with me. I know that look.* I wanted to apologize. *Wait a minute. You bet there is something wrong,* I thought. *You messed everything up last night. I don't care what you think.*

"Nothing," I said.

"You look deep in thought."

What are you, a mind reader? I thought. *Bug off! I won't do it again.*

"No, I was just thinking."

"Well, if you want to talk about it later, you know where I am."

"Okay," I said.

As Mike walked away I wanted to run after him and tell him how I felt, but how can you tell someone how you feel when you don't know how you feel? So I stood there and the war continued.

12

With a little over two weeks left to go in the season, everyone was waiting for Olympics to begin. We all knew the counselors were dividing the campers into the blue and red teams, which would compete in all types of events for one week. This year all the kids in my bunk were eligible to be chosen as camper captain of a team.

When I was a seven-year-old first-year camper, I'd dreamed of being a captain and leading my team on to victory. Last year at this time everybody, even some of the counselors, had said, "Richie, next year is your year to be captain." I would hang my head and feel sort of embarrassed whenever they said it, but deep inside I really wished it would come true. Sometimes during a boring math class I would picture myself running alongside the other camper captains holding high in my hand the flaming torch that would light the fire to start the games. Everyone in camp would be cheering. "Richie! Richie! Richie!"

"Richie, what's the answer to number six?" Mr. Singer, my math teacher, would interrupt.

"Richie! Richie! Richie!" I would raise both hands, fists clenched high to the sky, and then the index finger of my right hand would go up. My team was number one. I was number one.

"Number one," I would say. "The answer to number one, Mr. Singer?"

"No. Number six," Mr. Singer would say in disgust.

But that was only a memory, and now the real thing was about to happen. I hoped. I said "I hoped" because I was afraid to say I would definitely, for fear it would not come true.

I knew that Olympics had to start on either Monday, Tuesday, or Wednesday, but so did the people that were running the camp. So each year they would try and do things to make us think it would start and then tell us it was a fake-out. I was sure it would start at the all-camp swim meet on Monday. I told Fred, "Just you wait." No sooner had the words come out of my mouth than there was a tremendous explosion and counselors dressed as frogmen came up out of the lake. Soon they were joined by four other counselors dressed as soldiers. They ran around us, shouting and yelling. Then someone turned on the PA system and a deep voice said, "Welcome to the red and blue 1980 Olympics. This year promises to be the biggest and best Olympics ever. I know everyone has been waiting for the announcement of the camper captains."

I took a deep breath and I tried to swallow a big lump that had formed in my throat.

"The camper captains are, fake-out, fake-out, fake-out!"

"Damn it!" I muttered. "Why do they play games like that!"

Well, if it wasn't starting at the swim meet, I knew exactly when it would start. It would start tonight at evening activity. I could hardly eat my dinner that night. In just two hours I would be cap—I mean, I hoped to be captain.

When they called us to line up for evening activity, I was the first one out. I paced nervously until the rest of the guys came. Only a few more minutes.

The head counselor blew his whistle and everybody quieted down. He began to make a few announcements when it happened for real. Fireworks lit up the sky, spelling out Olympics 1980. Counselors, faces painted in red and blue, were running around throwing papers up in the air. Sirens and bells rang over the PA system, and we were all told to go to the rec hall to find out what teams we were on. I ran as fast as I could, yelling and screaming as I flew by everyone.

When I got to the rec hall, I saw that the outside was plastered with paper telling each camper which team they were on. I was on the red team with Fred, while John and Marty were on the blue. Once inside we separated, the red on the left side of the rec hall, the blue on the right.

My heart pounded wildly. The head counselor stood up in front of the teams and waited for silence.

"The camper captains for this year are, blue team, Amy Johnson and John Miller. And red team, Susan Simon and Fred . . ."

Everyone cheered and shouted. The captains came forward to get the torches. I patted Fred on the back as he ran by and I wished him luck. Inside I felt lousy. I wanted to cry and scream out, "Not fair, I should have been picked." I wanted to kick over a bench and break a window, but instead I followed my team. We ran behind the camper captains, who were on their way, with torch in hand, to start Olympics.

I really wasn't running very fast, and eventually almost everybody was ahead of me. I thought of turning around and running in the opposite direction. I stopped.

"You should have been picked for captain."

"Yeah, you should have been captain."

I turned around. It was Robby and Sally. *What a great brother and sister.*

"You were robbed," said Robby.

"Yeah, you were robbed," echoed Sally.

"I don't care who they picked—I still consider you the captain."

"Right. I agree with Robby. You're our captain."

I put my arms around them and gave both a hug. *They're really not that bad.*

"C'mon," I said, grabbing their hands. "Let's catch up to the team."

That night I could not fall asleep. This was probably the worst day in my life. It was worse than the time I was sick on my tenth birthday and the party had to be canceled. It was worse than the time I flunked my first test and had to take it home for my parents to sign. It was even worse than not getting elected president of my seventh-grade homeroom. At least I would have a chance to run for president in eighth grade, but the chance to be camper captain was gone forever.

I'm just as good as Fred, I thought. *In fact, I'm a better athlete. Why wasn't I picked? It wasn't fair.*

I could feel myself getting angry all over again. Then, I don't know why, I began to have a conversation with God. To myself, of course. *Why are you doing all this to me this year? You almost didn't let me get the bed I wanted and you put me in right field and you messed things up with me and girls and you let me get scared instead of Chuck. Did I do something wrong? Have I been bad? Is it something I said? Is it because I beat up my brother two weeks before camp? It was really his fault for coming into my room. Is it because I asked Paul for some answers on the nine weeks' test his class took before mine? I wasn't cheating, I was just checking things. Or was it because I called Chuck a nerd? It's not my fault you made him a nerd. Well, then what is it? What have I done for you to be so mean? Huh? Answer. Okay, be like that. Don't answer, see if I care. Damn it! It ain't fair. It just isn't.*

I don't think I slept a wink that night.

The next day before the first events began each captain called a team meeting. Susan and Fred stood up on benches in front of everyone and began to lead cheers. I sat by myself in the back off to one side. There was nothing for me to cheer about.

"I guess I owe you an explanation."

I looked up; it was Mike. I looked down.

"Come outside with me for a moment."

I wanted to say no or get lost, but I followed him

outside instead. As he sat down on the ground, he motioned for me to sit beside him. I sat down, but not that close. I stared at the ground.

"I guess you're wondering why you weren't picked to be captain."

I continued to stare at the ground.

"If we just went on your past record at camp, there wouldn't have been any question, but this year you are not a team person. You are a Richie-only person."

"Huh?" I said, looking up for only a moment.

"Remember when you didn't want to play right field? The only thing you were interested in was—"

"That's not true," I interrupted. "Right field is only for—"

"Only for what?" said Mike, sternly.

"Nothing," I said, and again I looked at the ground.

"See, that's what I mean. And you haven't let Chuck alone for one minute the whole season."

"I'm not the only one. The other guys do it too."

"But I expect more from you. You used to be a leader. People used to follow you instead of—"

"Are you finished?" I snapped. I didn't wait to hear Mike's answer. I got up and walked back to the rec hall. The cheers were still in progress so I returned to my seat in the corner.

Mike's words repeated themselves over and over again. *"You are a Richie-only person, not a team person. You used to be a leader. I expected more from you. You haven't let Chuck alone. You are a Richie-only person."*

When the cheers were over, I followed the team out of the rec hall. Mike was waiting outside the door, but I pretended not to see him.

"I expected more from you. You used to be a leader." I am a leader, I thought. *I expected more. I'm going to score so many points you'll wish you made me captain. I'll show you, Mike. You're wrong,* I thought.

The first event I was involved in was a swim meet. I was a pretty good swimmer, so I got to participate in three events—the fifty-yard butterfly stroke, the fifty-yard relay, and the diving. I was expected to win all three, but I lost the butterfly race by inches, had a false start that disqualified the relay team, and had awful form in most of my dives. I argued a little over the false-start call, but there was nothing I could say about the other two events.

On the second day of competition our basketball team was ahead by one point with less than thirty-five seconds to go in the game. All we had to do was hold on to the ball, but somehow I let a pass from Fred slip between my fingers and go out of bounds. To make matters worse, on the next play I fouled John as he was driving to the basket, and he made both foul shots, giving the game to blue by one point.

"Damn it, Richie!" yelled Fred. "The ball was right in your hands, what happened?"

"It just slipped out, Fred. I tried."

Fred gave me a you-lost-the-game look and walked away.

The afternoon of the fourth day we had our baseball game, and I was to play shortstop. I felt really good, and I was determined to make up for my poor showing so far. The first inning was scoreless, but in the bottom half of the second, the blue team got three consecutive hits. With the bases loaded, a perfect double-play ground ball came to me. I ran toward it, trying to pick it up on a short hop, but the ball slid under my glove and into left field, letting two runs score. The blue team scored one more run on a long fly ball and I was glad to see that inning end.

Fred pulled me aside on the bench when we got in. "Hey, Richie, what the hell is the matter with you?"

"The ball took a bad hop, Fred. It wasn't my fault."

"Bad hop, my eye. You misplayed it."

"I'd like to see you do better," I snapped back.

"I am doing better," he replied and walked away.

That inning I struck out, and I did it again in the fourth and in the sixth. Nevertheless, our team was able to score four runs, and we were leading four to three in the last half of the seventh inning. After the first two blue members made outs, the next three got on base. I was a little worried that they might score the winning runs, until I saw that the next batter was Chuck.

We've got this game in the bag. I watched Chuck swing wildly at two pitches that were out of the strike zone. For some reason he didn't swing at the next three pitches, so the count ran to three and two.

"Just lob it in," I said. "We'll get it."

The next pitch was right down the center of the plate. Chuck upper cut it wildly, causing the ball to go sky-high between short and third.

"I got it," I yelled to Fred.

"No, I got it," yelled Fred. "Stay away, Richie."

"It's mine, Fred, I called it."

By now Fred and I were face to face, and as we crashed into each other, we lost our balance and fell to the ground a split second before the ball did. In the confusion two runs scored and we lost 5 to 4.

"I told you I had it," yelled Fred. "It was mine all the way."

"The shortstop is supposed to call the play," I yelled back. "I had it, it was mine."

"You're a nerd, Richie! That's the second game you lost for our team. I should have put you in right field."

"Then why didn't you?"

"Maybe I will next time. You've changed, Richie. You're a real loser now."

The word loser rang in my head. Nobody calls me a loser and gets away with it.

"Come over here and say that," I said.

Fred started toward me, but we were quickly separated by our bunkmates.

Just because he's the captain, he thinks he's hot stuff. Well, he ain't.

When I got back to the bunk, Fred was already lying down on his bed. I lay down on my bed and didn't look in his direction. And when it looked as if he were about to talk to me, I turned my back on him and closed my eyes.

After dinner Mike pulled me aside.

"I want to talk to you," he said.

"Again? I heard what you said the other day."

"You never let me finish."

"Well, finish it then."

"Not here. I want to do this where we can be alone."

We walked up to the ball field, and he motioned for me to sit on the bleachers.

"I'd rather stand," I said.

"Suit yourself," said Mike. "I watched you play ball today. You seemed to be having a tough time."

"Did you see the grounder in the second inning?"

Mike nodded.

"It hit a rut in the field and slid under my glove. If it wasn't for that I would have had a double play."

"Yeah, it was a tough play."

"What about the fly ball? Wasn't it mine? Didn't Fred try to hog it?"

Mike listened but he didn't answer. Instead he put his arm around me and said, "No, Richie, it was Fred's ball."

I brushed Mike's hand off my shoulder and started to walk away.

"Wait, let me finish," said Mike.

I didn't want to stay. Couldn't Mike see he was making matters worse. First I wasn't picked for captain and now everything was going wrong.

"Richie, in all the years I've known you and watched you play in camp, I've never seen you choke in a pressure situation. This week you've done it three times. In the bunk you are snapping at everybody and bossing people around. It's just not like you."

"Everybody is entitled to a bad game or two. I'll do better tomorrow."

"I really believe you'll try to do better tomorrow,

just as you gave it your all today, but that's not the issue," said Mike.

"Then what is?" I asked.

"I think you're running away from your feelings."

"What are you talking about?"

"I think you're upset over the fact that you weren't chosen captain and Fred was, and I also think you're angry at me for what I said to you the other day."

I wanted to look Mike straight in the eye and deny what he said, but I felt my eyes beginning to get wet as I hung my head and said nothing. Thoughts flew around in my brain like several Super Balls bouncing off a wall: *I didn't have a false start in the swimming meet. I should have been picked. Fred's pass was bad and the ball was slippery. I feel angry, mad, furious, damn it, shit. Fred used to be my friend. No one in the bunk likes me anymore. Why wasn't I picked? This is the worst summer I ever had. I'm never coming back to camp again. I am a leader. I'm not the only one that ever picked on Chuck. I'm better than Fred. How can you be angry at your best friend? How can you be angry at the counselor you looked up to. Damn it. Damn it. Damn it.*

We both stood there for what seemed to be an eternity.

Mike got up and put his arm around me again, and we walked back to the bunk. Just before we walked in the door I wanted to say something to Mike but nothing came out. Mike smiled and squeezed my arm. I still felt a little mad.

13

After my talk with Mike I really thought I would do better. But it didn't happen, at least not right away.

During the football game the next day, I dropped a pass. I was a little afraid to go back to the huddle because I was sure Fred would say, "Starting again, huh, Richie. You were in the clear, why did you drop the ball?" Instead, he patted me on the back and said, "Good try, you'll get it next time."

You know it's a funny thing, but after Fred said that to me I felt worse. It really wasn't a very good try. I should have had it. Hit me right in the hands, and don't coaches say, "If it hits you right in the hands, you should catch it." I should have caught it. There were no more passes thrown to me before halftime. It was just as well, because I probably would have dropped them also. Late in the third quarter Fred told me to go five steps down the middle and cut to the left and he would place the ball right in my gut. In choose-up games Fred and I had worked this play to perfection. As I lined up waiting for the ball to be snapped, I imagined myself as a tight end playing in the Super Bowl. The commentators up in the booth had their field glasses trained on me, in anticipation.

"Well, Mel, Richie hasn't really played that well, but it's just a matter of time."

"That's right, Jack. You certainly can't contain someone as great as him for very long. Back to you, Jack, for the play-by-play."

"The ball snaps and Fred fades back to pass. Richie has broken free up the middle and he cuts to the left. The ball is a little high, but he leaps up and makes a spectacular catch. Ohhh baby, what a grab! That's the ole Richie we knew!"

"That's right, Jack, if we could look at it again on replay, watch that great move . . ."

Hup two, hup three. I charged up the middle and on five I cut to the left. I saw the ball spiraling toward me. I felt the ball hit me in my fingertips. I still felt the ball in my fingertips. I still felt the ball in my fingertips. Oh, my God, I caught the ball!

"Run, Richie, run!" the crowd cheered, as I cut back to the right and started up the field.

John caught me from behind, but not till I gained fifteen yards. During the rest of the game I caught two more passes and had one interception and our team went on to win, 14 to 7.

As I walked off the field, out of the corner of my eye I caught Mike smiling in my direction. On the way down to the bunk, Fred caught up with me and began to chatter about something. I nodded my head and looked interested, but in reality I wasn't paying much attention. I was still angry at him because he had been chosen captain. I was still angry at myself for being angry at him for being chosen captain. I still hoped, beyond all hope, that someone would say that a dreadful mistake had been made and I was really the one that was supposed to be captain, but I knew deep down inside that it would never happen, and I wondered if I could ever be friends with Fred again like we were before. That thought made me sad.

A special Olympic version of capture the flag was the last event. Each team had to hide and protect their own flag while trying at the same time to capture the other team's flag. The game lasted forty-five minutes, and the team won that scored the most points (one point for each enemy team member captured) or captured the other team's flag and returned safely to base. After six days of competition only two points separated the teams. The winner of this event would also be the winner of Olympics.

Just before the game started Fred met with our team to map out some strategy. As he talked, I pictured myself snatching the enemy flag and running toward home base with forty blue-team members following in hot pursuit. Two rocks blocked my path ahead and there was no alternate route. I accelerated as I approached the rocks, and just six inches before them I took a giant leap. I sailed thirty feet into the air and landed upright on home base. The gallery of red-team members waiting there broke loose and I was hoisted up on their shoulders and carried around camp. Everyone was chanting, "RICHIE, RICHIE, RICHIE."

"Richie? Richie?"

"Huh," I said.

"Come on, Richie," said Fred. "The game is about to start."

When the whistle blew, I ran straight to the rec hall and climbed up on the roof. From here I had a clear view of the whole playing area, but what I saw puzzled me at first. The blue team had placed most of their members at the far end of the camp while Chuck stood alone in the woods at the near end. At first I thought Chuck was lost, but then I realized what they had done. They wanted our team to think that their flag was where most of their people were, but in fact it was being guarded solely by Chuck. I could see that most of the red-team members had been fooled by this trick, and I knew I had little time to lose.

I walked over to the edge of the roof to climb down, but I saw two blue members standing and talking under the drainpipe I would use. Quietly, like a commando, I crawled on my stomach to the other side of the roof. A tree branch about two feet away stood between me and safety. I knew that if I were to take a running start the blue-team members would hear me and I would be caught. Yet I wasn't sure I could make it if I tried to jump toward the tree from a stationary position. As I was pondering what to do, the loudspeaker blared out, "There are now thirty minutes left." If I was going to jump, I had to do it now. I squatted down on the edge of the roof like a coil ready to spring. "Please," I said, looking up toward the heavens, "if you are busy doing anything now that needs your total concentration, please let me know. Otherwise, if it's not too much trouble, could you please make sure I get to the tree." There were no crashes of thunder or lightning so I threw my arms upward, catapulting myself toward the tree limb. I reached it easily, but no sooner had I landed, than I heard a big crack and the limb began to sag. Again I looked upward. "I hate to ask you for two favors in a row, but . . ." I never finished because the limb seemed to stop sagging.

As I began to move slowly, hand over hand, to the main trunk, I heard voices below me and I froze. Two members of the blue team had come

around the corner of the rec hall and were directly below me. I hung for what seemed like hours. Finally they left, and I made it quickly to the main trunk and down. I took a back way through the woods and got to within twenty feet of Chuck without being seen. He had his back to me and from here it would be easy to steal the flag and race for home. My daydream was on the verge of coming true. I crawled ten more feet on my stomach. Chuck still had his back to me. Fifteen minutes to go. I raised my head to see exactly where the flag was and saw Fred crawling up on the other side of Chuck one hundred and eighty degrees across from me.

Suddenly, without warning, Chuck turned and stared in my direction. I froze. Chuck took two steps toward me. *I've got to hold my breath. Two steps more. If he can't see me now, he's blind.* I looked over and saw that Fred was no more than fifteen feet from the flag. *No glory for me this year.*

"I got you!" yelled Chuck. "You're my prisoner."
No sense running, I thought. *I'm sunk.*

I stood up and picked up my arms. But Chuck had already turned around and was running toward Fred. He caught Fred off guard, and as Fred turned to run, he tripped over his own feet and fell into the bushes. Chuck jumped on top of him and easily captured him. In the confusion I got the flag and was on my way toward home base before Chuck knew what happened. As I started toward the finish line, I wondered how he could have missed me. *Boy! What a dummy! He was looking right at me. If I were in his place and he were in mine, he wouldn't have gotten away. I would have definitely caught him. The only way I could have gotten away was if he . . . I mean the only way he could have gotten away was if I let him get away purposely. He let me go. That turkey let me go. He had to. He was looking right at me.* I ran toward the base and all the reds rushed up to meet me. They lifted me high in the air and cheered. In the distance I saw Chuck looking over his shoulder at me as he walked toward his team. I mouthed the word thanks and waved. I think he was too far away to see it. Maybe he wasn't.

14

Everyone has always told me that girls are more mature than boys. I think they are wrong. Take the last week of camp, for example. That was the week of all the special events. One night we floated lit candles on the lake and made wishes. A lot of the girls cried. When I asked them, "Why are you crying?" they said, "Because we're happy. We had such a good summer."

And the last night of camp, after the banquet, the same girls cried again. This time they said they were sad to see camp end. This is being mature? Now, don't get me wrong, I didn't want camp to end either, but I wasn't going to cry about it. I gave up crying when I was six years old. None of the guys in the bunk cried after the banquet, not even Chuck.

Since it was our last night, we folded up all the metal beds and put them in a pile in the corner. Then we put all of our mattresses in the center of the floor, and we stayed up all night and talked. I heard more great jokes that night than ever before. John told one about the book *How to Kiss Girls by Mr. Completely*. Fred asked, "Why did the chicken cross the road?" And the answer was, "For some fowl reason." Marty told one about the two cannibals who were talking and one said, "I hate my mother-in-law." And the other one said, "Then, just eat your vegetables."

After we got tired of telling jokes, we had an elimination wrestling match. I was one of the last four, but I got pinned by Marty and he eventually went on to win.

Then somebody suggested that we go to the girls' cabin and scare them. I knew Mike heard our plans, but since it was the last night, I guess he didn't care, because he pretended to be asleep when we left.

It's pretty difficult to keep everyone quiet and to-gether, but somehow we managed to get to the girls' bunk without getting caught. We crept slowly up the cabin steps, and as we flung open the door, we all yelled "Surprise!" Unfortunately, the only ones who were surprised were us. The bunk was com-pletely empty except for the counselors, who were laughing hysterically.

"What's so funny?" we asked. "Where are the girls?"

It took the counselors about two minutes to stop laughing.

"The girls decided to go visit your bunk about ten minutes ago. They are probably there now."

All of us tore out of the girls' bunk and ran back to our bunk as fast as we could, but by the time we got there, Mike told us that the girls had already left. By this time it was three o'clock in the morning, and I guess I fell asleep because the next thing I knew, I was being awakened for breakfast.

After breakfast we carried our things up to the athletic field and waited for the buses to arrive. My bus arrived before Fred's, so I said my final good-byes.

"Will you be back next year, Richie?"

"I guess so. How about you?"

"I'll be back for sure. You know next year we have the honor of waiting on tables."

"Yeah, what a job. I hope I get a girls' table to wait on. Younger boys are such slobs. We were never like that when we were their age."

"Yeah, I know what you mean."

"We really had a great year, didn't we?" I shook Fred's hand.

"We sure did. Listen, Richie, a word of advice. Don't get into any rowboats with Chuckie over the winter."

"Very funny, very funny. Listen, Fred, have a good year."

"You too, Richie."

I picked up my bag and started to walk toward the bus. Over my shoulder I caught a glimpse of Chuck following me. I slowed up a little, and we both reached the door at the same time. I let him get on first and I followed. Halfway down the aisle he stopped and looked back at me. The only places left were on the back seat.

"I guess you'll have to sit back there with us," I said. *But that doesn't mean you can sit here next year,* I thought.

Chuck didn't say anything, but he almost smiled. So did I.